Choose

Anne Congiu

First published in 2020

Copyright © 2020 Anne Congiu

ISBN 978-0-6482593-2-9

Cover design: Busybird Publishing

Layout and typesetting: Busybird Publishing

For Emilio

Acknowledgements

I am thankful and lucky to be supported by a wonderful group of writers, family and friends. Their continuous encouragement, feedback and interest in my writing ignites my creativity, and spurs me to conjure up ideas that I can then in turn put to paper. In particular I am fortunate to have the support from Lynnie Mary Kincaid. Her guidance has been invaluable.

But above all, I am most grateful that I had a father who treasured the love of reading and writing. He left more than fifty diaries, one for each of his last fifty living years, and many short stories, voice recordings and poems. He spent most of his time at his desk, especially in his senior years, after entering late retirement. His desk was his sanctuary and he protected it as his most valued house item. Under lock and key, we were only permitted to read his writings after he passed away, some fifteen years ago. And I find it sad that, now in my senior years, I fully understand the love he had, mine perhaps not as much as his, but love, just the same.

A mother's love for her children is unconditional, with each child loved equally. When placed in a situation where she has to choose one child over another, how does she do this? And can she?

Autumn 2008

With kettle whistling loudly, and tea bag dropped into her old mug, a calmness engulfs her. Almost in robotic form, she pours the boiling water, stirs, and taps the teaspoon twice on the rim. Maintaining a tight grip on the handle, she carries the cup through the hallway, pushes open the fly-wire door with her foot and, dangling her tea bag, makes her way outside. She doesn't pick up her book from the hallstand this time. She doesn't care to today.

Ignoring her comfy hammock, she snugly wraps her dressing gown around her body, lifts up the collar and side-sits on the porch railing. With her head barely missing the hanging basket, she supports her back on the corner post and slurps her first sip.

Mesmerised by the translucent dancing leaves of the Japanese maple, she stares outward. The old maple that her mother planted all those years ago, now so much a part of her front garden, providing serenity and privacy when she sits and hides behind it. But now, with its autumn foliage almost stripped, she doesn't have the privacy she yearns for.

The sun slowly brightening the morning, she relishes seeing the wake of a new day. Swaying to a gentle breeze, the last of the defiant leaves hang on and the weak ones detach, gracefully falling to the ground, laying silently amongst the others fallen before them. And as she stares down at them, she thinks of her own lifecycle, of her parents and grandparents; growing, maturing, living, before retreating to the soil. With the falling leaves signalling winter is approaching, she silently smiles in contentment.

She delights on how truly beautiful Mount Beauty is in autumn as the changing tones of reds, oranges and yellows befall to a welcoming bareness of winter's shimmery greys and whites. The driving force for her parents to choose this place was its picturesque winter scape, and the abundant rainfall feeding and energising a constant greenery and nurture for the ground and all living things. The openness of expansive farmlands and its closeness to the High Country and surrounds reminded her father of his parents' much-loved homeland in northern Europe. And even though he himself had never been there, the stories his father told him and his brother Brian were vivid in his mind.

The close-knit community welcomed and encouraged the young family into their fold, and she reflects on this magical place — now all just for her.

Before taking another sip, she lifts up the tea bag, squishes it between her two fingers, and tosses it into the garden bed in front of her. Legs dangling, she's pulled further outward, past the letterbox, across the road, and into the wooded area. It saddens her to see the spread of new homes snaking into the woods, almost caterpillar-like, munching up everything in their way, replacing old trees and foliage with bricks and mortar. Even though she has lived here practically all her life, and has stared into the woods every morning, each day displays a new picture. She sees old plants die and watches new growth push upward, protruding through the canopy in search of the sun, effortlessly embracing new life.

With her hand cupped tightly around the bottom of the cup, to extract the last bit of warmth before sipping the last drop, she's absorbed in a dreamlike state of tranquillity. As the sun breaks, welcoming the start of the weekday routine, children on bikes head off to school and neighbours walk their dogs. Old-time neighbours wave and nod with a friendly, 'Morning, Aida', but new neighbours awkwardly walk on, almost frightened of her, or frightened of the story they have heard; the story she carries. If she closes her eyes, she relives the past, the happy and the sad, but she dares not go there now.

Then something catches her eye as she peers through the maple. There's an image ahead in the distance. As the tree branches sway, it disappears, but it reappears as they sway back.

A shadowy figure of a person — a man, she thinks. With her eyes gazing over her cup, she squints to focus as he comes closer. A sudden fear engulfs her. It's not an illusion, or a shadow, it's an actual person heading towards the house, and she can tell he's not a local by the strange look about him. With dead leaves swishing around his ankles as he casually walks on the path, he slightly bends his head to the side to dodge the overhangs. As he gets closer, she can clearly make out his pale jeans, black sneakers, sloppy t-shirt and hands swaying loosely by his side. He takes a quick glance at the mobile phone in his hand before tucking it into his back pocket.

But in an instant, as he approaches the road, he takes a sharp right, and heads towards town, intermingling with the children and people walking their dogs, and is encapsulated amongst them.

Oh, what a strange feeling. She shudders as she tightens her robe around her chest. For a second she thought their eyes had met. She is left bemused as she recalls all the other false sightings, with this one also smothering a flutter of hope that she has been craving for so many years.

Her legs slowly return to the gentle sway in harmonised rhythm, as her head leans back on the post, still clutching her now cold, empty cup. Closing her eyes, she returns to her tranquil state and, unwittingly, recounts her past.

******

Spring 1978

Moving into a new town is exciting. They are so glad to get away from the 'big smoke'. Life will be easy, they pray. The community and neighbours welcome them warmly, as country people do and, as they breathe in the country air, they are full of optimism to live the life they have dreamed and planned for themselves and their young family.

'It's the right move,' they reassure themselves.

'There's the old gum tree on the corner of Edge Street,' yells Marlene in excitement, nudging Nick to turn in.

'Yes. I know, Marlene,' he replies, remembering the many times they visited, as they waited for their offer on the house to be accepted.

The shimmering sun on the silvery bark of the old tree signals a left turn off Western Highway. They are even more excited as the heavy-loaded, old station wagon, bouncing along the dusty, pebbled side road, edges closer to their new home.

With the car window now fully wound down, Marlene flicks her auburn wavy hair away from her face, sits her sunglasses on top of her head, and glues her big, brown eyes on the road ahead. Grasping the windowsill tightly with both hands, she turns her head as they pass the first, second and third letterboxes of their neighbours.

'One. Three. Five,' she counts out loud.

Their letterbox soon comes into sight. A large number seven painted on the tin box, precariously hanging on the weathered picket fence. She sees overgrown grasses gnawing through the entry gate covering and crowding the broken, uneven concrete path and weather-beaten wooden steps to the porch. Her mind swarms with ideas on how to make this a warm country entrance.

The old timber bungalow with its bullnose verandah, supported on thick hardwood stumps, stands high off the ground with ample clearance on all sides from neighbouring boundaries. Past its abandoned, unruly stature she sees a proud, dignified, cloaked building waiting to be uncloaked and, more importantly, lived in and loved.

Situated just out of town, but in comfortable walking distance to the centre and schools, the charm of this property is its north-facing position, opposite the beautiful woods. Mystical in many ways, when she closes her eyes and takes a deep breath, she inhales all the different fragrances of eucalypts, and a wide variety of native bushes, tall swaying grasses and wild flowers.

'Wake up, kids. Here we are,' she says, just as Nick pulls on the brake, turns off the engine and flips up the sun visor. He throws his arms on the steering wheel to relax his shoulders and, with wide eyes peering upward, takes a few minutes to stare at the house.

Marlene jumps out, opens the back door for the kids, stands back and looks up.

'Perfect,' she whispers. 'Just perfect.'

Impatiently foraging through her handbag, she finds the keys and makes her way to the front door with Nick closely behind her. With a big sigh, she turns the key and flings the door open.

'It's so dusty,' she says. But with the huge smile on her face, Nick can tell she's pleased.

The children follow behind them. Slowly and cautiously they wander around to inspect each room and, in no time, Alex and Aida race upstairs.

Marlene's mind is immediately focussed on which rooms to clean first. The lounge at the front of the house on the left is fairly clean, with just a bit of dusting and vacuuming required. The thick hardwood floorboards, in perfect condition, only need a damp mop over them, and the rug, ragged and thin, 'Can be tossed out,' she says to herself.

She walks to the window, pulls away the curtain and looks out. 'Errkk,' she screeches, as she looks at the porch covered in spider webs, cluttered with old, broken pots and dried-out hanging baskets, and quickly draws the curtain back.

Turning into the hallway to the right, she enters the large kitchen and dining room, where it seems most of the cleaning needs to be done. She looks again, then looks away and rolls her eyes as she makes a mental note of all the work she has ahead of her.

Back into the hallway. Past the central stairway towards the back of the house is a small laundry room with a toilet, also in much need of cleaning, and two small rooms, large enough to provide storage to the many boxes that will soon be arriving in the removalist's truck.

Making her way up the stairs to the right of the landing is the huge master bedroom with a large window. She glances up to the high ceiling and admires the delicately decorated rosette in the centre and the intricate cornices, just as she remembers them when they first inspected the house. She can stare at this forever, but is pulled towards the half-open window. With the soft breeze swaying the curtains, she looks out to the uninterrupted view of the woods across the road.

'How peaceful.' She sighs. 'How beautiful.'

'This is my room,' shouts Alex, bursting into the room.

'Oh no, it's not. This is Mum and Dad's room. Yours is over there,' she replies, pointing to the room opposite hers.

'Oh, wow, Mum. This is cool.' Alex gasps as he runs in to inspect it.

'And my room, Mummy, which is my room?' asks Aida.

'This one, Aida. This one next to Alex. Of course, Mummy has to clean it up, but it will be really nice once we've finished. You'll see.'

Behind the master bedroom is a smallish spare bedroom, 'For guests,' she mutters, and at the end of the hallway is the bathroom.

'Why don't you both go and inspect the garden?' She barely has time to finish the sentence and Alex and Aida race downstairs into the back yard.

'There's lots of garden for the children to play in,' she says as she joins Nick to make their way outside.

An old, timber shed sits at the back of the garden.

'Large enough to house the car, once it's cleared out,' she says to Nick.

Holding on to the side of the shed, she stands on her tippy toes and peers over the back fence to see an abandoned vacant block, with overgrown, dense bushes.

'Oh, dear. I wonder who owns this big parcel of land?' she asks herself.

Heading back inside, down the hallway and out the front door, Marlene and Nick start to bring in boxes from the boot of the car.

'Come on, kids. Come and help,' she yells, just as she turns her head and sees the removalist truck pull up. 'Nick. The removalists are here. Quick. Come give them a hand.'

She contemplates everything that has to be done, once the furniture has all been delivered and placed in the relevant rooms.

'Gosh, there is so much to do,' she whispers to herself.

But with a smile of satisfaction, they eagerly get the bedrooms cleaned and set up as first priority, and then focus on the kitchen.

'Thank goodness the lino is in good condition,' she says to Nick. 'But we'll have to replace the lino in the bathroom.'

Nick nods in agreement.

The tidying, cleaning and reshuffling of furniture tires them and it is heavenly to throw themselves into bed at the end of a very long day.

'I'm exhausted,' says Marlene.

'Me too,' says Nick.

With the excited children now bathed and tucked into bed, Nick and Marlene wrap their arms around each other and drift heavily into sleep. They don't notice there are no street lights lighting up the bedroom. Nor do they hear the slow woo-hoo noise of the owls perched high in the dead, hollow gum trees across the road. The first day in this beautiful country town coming to a close, and signalling the start of a new beginning.

And how peaceful it is to wake with birds hovering and chirping around the garden as the sun pours into the house. All their aches and pains from the previous day seem to be soothed in these new surroundings.

The days that follow are spent re-positioning furniture around the rooms. It has to be just right for Marlene.

'No! Here, Nick. It's better here,' she says, pointing her finger in the direction of the lounge window. 'I'll be able to see the garden with it here.'

'Make up your mind, Marlene. This heavy shifting is killing me,' he snaps.

Marlene knows it will take time to fully settle in, but she can feel the slow country pace engulfing her already.

******

Chapter 1

As Marlene finishes unpacking, and with the children playing outside, Nick makes his way into town. His signature on the office lease barely dry, he opens the glass door, takes a deep sigh and walks through the reception area, down the short hallway to his office, first door on the left. He inspects the small kitchen behind his office, before unlocking the back door leading onto the lane, then drives his car around and unloads the boxes from the boot. A heavy tool kit, mop, broom and small box of cleaning supplies are carried inside. Letting out a heavy sigh, he contemplates all the work he has ahead of him.

Broken-down shelving is unhinged, carried outside and piled against the back brick wall. Nick neatly leans it against the building in readiness to cart to the tip. His handyman experience comes into good use for the big opening next week.

He is hopeful to acquire customers in and around the community and, more importantly, to build their trust and friendship. He can't wait to hang up his certificate with the new registered name, and to greet customers from near and far.

He opens the front door. 'Let some fresh air in,' he says, and secures it against the wall with the recently delivered White and Yellow Pages telephone books, still wrapped in plastic.

Stepping down to the footpath, over the ditch and onto the street, with his hands on his hips, he glances left to right and admires his office location. The footpath high off the road lifts the buildings, which can be seen unobstructed from street view. Standing back, almost in the middle of the road, he sees the Mount Beauty Newsagent on his left and Jack's Legal Services on the right.

'Great spot,' he says. 'Great spot!'

Rolling up his sleeves on his old, worn shirt hanging loose over his jeans, he makes many trips to the car to carry in more boxes.

And the next day is also spent cleaning, with his focus now fully on the business. After all, they will need money coming in before they spend all their savings.

He paints the reception area a light blue and replaces old vinyl flooring with new vinyl tiles, bought from Jim's Mount Beauty General Store up the road. He washes and wipes down walls and gives the toilet a good scrub. 'This'll do,' he whispers to himself. The tiny kitchen also gets a thorough clean. The rest of the week is spent going around town, picking up office supplies and meeting the other shop owners.

Upon returning to the office one afternoon, he is surprised by the phone ringing.

'Hello! Oh! Yes. Yes. Thank you very much for connecting it so quickly,' he says to the Telecom lady on the other end of the line. He can't wait to get home to tell Marlene that the phone is connected. He is so excited.

******

Chapter 2

Grandma Edna and Grandpa Bill visit to give them a hand settling in. The children, especially Aida, love having their grandparents visit.

'It's a charming house, Marlene,' says Edna, once she's gone over all the rooms.

'It's just right for us, Mum.'

Aida is keen to show her grandma her bedroom. Her little hand waves as she points to every corner of the room and every piece of furniture, in particular her doll collection all neatly piled up in the pram under the window.

'It's beautiful, Aida,' says a proud grandma with a big smile on her face.

Once Edna and Bill settle in, Aida spends no time in putting on her smock so she can help her grandma in the kitchen. Whilst standing on the chair pulled up to the table, they bake her favourite chocolate cupcakes.

'Be careful you don't fall, dear,' says Bill.

'I won't, Grandpa. I'm a big girl now,' responds Aida, totally engrossed in the chore her grandma has given her. Clenching the back of the chair with one hand she turns around, and with the other she holds up her spread-out fingers and says, 'I'm nearly five, Grandpa, nearly five'.

He gives out a wholehearted chuckle, as he proudly throws a glance up at Edna.

With Bill in poor health, spending most of his time in the lounge room reading the newspaper or taking a nap, Edna spends her time with the children in the garden and also wanders into town to visit Nick in his office.

And as soon as the house is in good order, and Edna and Bill see that their daughter and family have settled in comfortably, they decide to return home.

'But you've only been here a few days,' says Marlene. 'The kids would love to have you stay longer.'

'Your father has appointments at the doctor, Marlene. We really need to get back. I'm so happy for you. This is a beautiful little town, just like you described it,' says Edna, looking at her only child with loving eyes. 'We'll see you soon, love.'

'Yes, Mum. Come on, kids. Come and give Grandma and Grandpa a hug.'

Alex and Aida come running in from outside and do indeed give their grandparents a tight hug. Standing on her tippy toes, Aida gives her grandma an extra-long hug.

'Drive carefully,' says Marlene, as they get into their car.

'We will, dear, we will.'

The kids run behind the car to Main Street and watch it drive off until it's no longer in sight, before running back to the garden to continue playing.

Early the next morning as Nick leaves for the office, with Alex on his bike and Aida by her side, Marlene ventures out, hoping to meet the neighbours. Those who are in their front yard nod a shy hello and Sandy next door stops to have a chat.

'Hello. I'm Sandy' she says, stretching out her hand to Marlene.

'Oh, hi, Sandy. I'm so pleased to finally meet you. I'm Marlene and this is Alex and Aida. We have seen you in your front garden, but we've been so busy settling in,' responds Marlene, as she gently shakes Sandy's hand.

Alex and Aida are eager to make friends with Sandy's little boy.

'I totally understand, Marlene. This is Max,' says Sandy, gesturing to her son, noticing that Alex and Aida are excited to meet him.

'Hello, Max,' replies Marlene.

Alex and Aida aren't shy, but Max is, and he slowly retreats and hides behind his mum's legs. Both Sandy and Marlene giggle.

'He'll be okay once he gets to know you,' assures Sandy.

'How old are you, Alex? And you, Aida?' asks Sandy.

'I'm six and a half,' says Alex.

'And I'm nearly five,' says Aida, holding her five fingers up to Sandy, just like she did to her grandpa.

'Oh, Aida, you are almost the same age as Max. He is already five,' says Sandy, swishing her blow-away hair from her face.

They exchange the usual chitter-chatter of where they've come from, a quick run-down of the town and neighbours, and how delightful the weather is. The conversation is polite and friendly, as Marlene expects. She finds out that Sandy works part-time at the local bakery.

'Just enough to see us through,' Sandy adds, and invites them to pop in when they're next in town.

Marlene tells Sandy that Nick is setting up his accountancy business and Sandy is very excited for them.

'Next to Jack's, the solicitor,' says Marlene.

'I'm sure he'll do well, Marlene. We need an accountant here. We don't want to keep driving up to Bright all the time,' Sandy says with a chuckle.

'Thank you, Sandy. I know Nick is putting his heart and soul into this new venture. Well, we'll see you again soon, Sandy. It is so nice to meet you. Goodbye, Max,' says Marlene, keen to get going.

'Goodbye,' responds Sandy, with Max still hiding behind her legs.

And with a quick wave, Marlene, Alex and Aida cross the road and take the tight path through the woods.

'Watch out for the hanging branches and the fallen logs on the path,' shouts Marlene.

But the kids are already dodging them as they plough on in front of her.

She stops to admire the different shrubs and wild spring flowers protruding through the long grasses as she waves her hand over them. The afternoon sun streams bright through the gum tree canopies and her face is soothed by the light wind on her face.

As they walk deeper, they come to a clearing, totally dry and barren, as if someone has come in with a brush cutter and cut everything down. The sun belting down onto the dry grass makes the day seem hotter than it actually is.

'What a great picnic spot. We can come and have our lunches here,' she says to the children.

With a little more confidence and excitement, the children run ahead of her, picking up dry leaves and throwing them up in the air above their heads, before they race back home, giggling all the way.

Alex spends the rest of the day casually riding his bike along the footpath to the end of the road and back. Aida plays on the front steps, counting them as she jumps up, down and then up again. When she sees her mum settled in the hammock looking outward, breathing in the fresh air, she sneaks up and plays peek-a-boo with her, popping up and under the hammock. It is so peaceful and tranquil, Marlene wonders why they hadn't thought of moving here earlier.

******

Chapter 3

'I don't think I'll need the car to get to work, Marlene. I'll leave it here in case you need it,' Nick says, as he rinses his cup under the tap and gets ready for work. 'It's such a lovely walk into town, and a great opportunity for me to meet the neighbours along the way, too.'

'That will allow us to drive around the township and discover the surrounds. Thanks, Nick.'

'Wow. This is great. You've done such a great job getting it to this stage so quickly, Nick,' says Marlene, when she visits him at his office the next day with the children. 'I'll bring in some pot plants to put by the front window. That'll fill in the space a bit.'

Glancing up at the wall, Marlene moves close to inspect Nick's business certificate, now framed and proudly hanging behind the reception desk. 'Bennet's Accounting,' she whispers proudly.

'Did you see the signage on the front window? Do you like it? Can you see it from the street as you are coming up?' Nick cannot contain his excitement and is talking so fast, Marlene doesn't get a chance to answer him.

'Slow down, Nick,' she says putting her hand over his mouth.

'Yes. You can see it just as you turn into Main Street. It's a great position, next to Jack's. It does look great, Nick, really does.'

The prospects are endless, they both admit. The only accountant in town.

'What a great opportunity,' Nick acknowledges. 'And the other shopkeepers are all very pleasant and very friendly. They've wished me well, Marlene,' he says smiling. 'And I know they mean it.'

Marlene's face gleams as she looks him straight in the eyes, almost trance-like. She studies his face, and cherishes this moment, realising just how much she loves him. As she keeps staring, she can see his boyish looks, hidden behind a grown, mature man. Thick dark hair, bushy eyebrows, thick smiley lips and sparkly eyes. She sees so much of him in Alex, and her heart explodes with love for this man, the father of her children. For a second she closes her eyes and takes a deep breath to absorb it all.

'I've distributed leaflets to the surrounding shops.' He continues. 'The locals walk past and wave when they see me behind the front desk and some have already enquired about my services. Isn't that fantastic? I've met Jack next door. He popped in to introduce himself. Such an awesome bloke. He's been here for a few years. Knows the place like the back of his hand he said.' Nick chuckles.

'That's wonderful,' responds Marlene, still gleaming with pride.

'Do you think you can pop these into the neighbour's letterboxes on your way back home?' he asks, as he hands her a handful of leaflets.

'Let's do as Daddy says, kids. Here. Take some leaflets. You can help me.'

And with a quick goodbye, Marlene and the children head out the door.

Feeling much more settled at home, Marlene, Alex and Aida wander into town almost daily. They love to pop into all the shops, introduce themselves and buy supplies, not just to stock up, but to show support for the locals. They go into the bakery store to say hello to Sandy, who insists on giving them a bag of fresh bread rolls to take home.

'Here, Marlene. Take these.'

The bag is shoved into Marlene's hand before she can reply.

And as they leave the smell of fish and chips two doors up lures them in to buy lunch.

'Hey, Nick. Here are some fish and chips for lunch,' Marlene shouts as they make their way into Nick's office.

'Leave them on the kitchen table, Marlene. Too busy now.'

'Okay. Bye,' she shouts. 'We'll see you at home tonight.'

It isn't long before the rest of the furniture and office equipment is delivered to the office. After a quick wipe down, Nick spends his time emptying boxes and filling up the filing cabinet and cupboards with essentials.

He is so excited to inspect the ad he placed in the local paper when he gets home and flicks through to the back pages where all the advertisements are placed.

'Look, Marlene. Here it is. I hope this promotes interest,' he says with a deep sigh. 'With no other accountant in town, and with luck, there should be customers from surrounding towns, too.' He rubs his hands in delight.

It all looks and feels too good to be true. They feel truly blessed with this new start.

******

Chapter 4

'Good morning, Sandy,' says Marlene as she arrives at the letterbox to check for mail the following day.

'Hi, Marlene. Beautiful day, isn't it? All settled in now?'

'Oh, getting there,' says Marlene. 'There's still so much stuff in boxes we haven't opened yet.'

'I've only been here a short time myself,' Sandy says. 'I'm so glad you've moved in next door. The house has been vacant for a while, so it's good for Max and I to finally have neighbours.'

'And where were you before, Sandy?' asks Marlene, casually removing spider webs around the letterbox with her finger.

'Oh, we've moved around a bit. We've actually come down from Townsville, then moved to Bega in New South Wales for a while, before making our way to the High

Country. Nick thought it would be good to settle here in Mount Beauty.'

'Nick?'

'Nick is Max's dad. What a coincidence that the kids' dads are both named Nick,' says Sandy, laughing. 'He'll join us as soon as he can. When he's finished his job up in Queensland, he'll come on down, he said.'

Marlene doesn't want to pry, and let's Sandy do all the talking, whilst she looks for more spider webs to pick at. Marlene is not convinced that Sandy is truly happy with these arrangements and somehow feels sorry for her. A young woman raising a child on her own is not easy. Having moved quite a few times in his short life probably explains why Max is so shy of strangers. But they seem to have settled comfortably into their little rental home and the locals are very supportive of her.

Continuing with a nervous laugh, Sandy says, 'He gets itchy feet, my Nick. He's like that, you know. But Max likes it here so I hope we can stay. And now with you as neighbours, I'd hate to have to move again.'

'No doubt then Max and Aida will be in the same class at school. Aida will be five soon,' says Marlene, changing the subject.

'Yes, I'm sure they will be. I have already enrolled him into Mount Beauty Primary. From what I hear, it seems like a nice school,' Sandy says.

'He is tall for his age.' Marlene leans on the fence. Sandy stands by the footpath keeping a sharp eye on Max playing across the road with Alex and Aida.

'Yes. Just like his father. He certainly didn't take after me.' She laughs.

Solidly built, with a dark mop of thick, short cut hair, in contrast to Sandy's fair curly locks, Marlene gets a vague impression of what Max's father may look like. Almost the same as Alex and Nick; father and son very much alike, whereas Aida has Marlene's features.

As the clouds start to roll in and cover the sun, both Marlene and Sandy look up and know it's time to go inside.

'Come on, Max. Time to come home now,' yells Sandy, as she tucks her hair securely behind her ears.

'You too, kids,' joins in Marlene.

On the other side at number nine are a quiet, elderly couple, who are polite and wave when they make eye contact, but make their way inside before Marlene can get a chance to chat with them.

She later finds out from Sandy that they have lived in the Mount Beauty surrounds most of their life, and are very well known to the locals, but due to ailing health have downsized from farm acreage to this smaller home in town.

'They're the Robinsons,' says Sandy. 'They like to keep to themselves, but seem nice enough. Mr Robinson doesn't venture out much these days, and it's mostly Mrs Robinson who tends to the garden when it's a nice day.'

At number eleven live Wayne and Marg Fernsby, a middle-aged couple, with their son Edward. They have the large corner block, so it's hard to see the neighbours next to them, around the corner, but Marlene is confident she'll get to meet them all, in time.

Alex wastes no time in making friends with Edward.

'Mum. Ed likes to play cricket, too. And he has a cool bike that goes much faster than mine.'

Marlene laughs and is pleased her son has made friends with someone close to home.

On the weekends, when Ed isn't at school, he and Alex ride their bikes everywhere in and around town, but best of all, they share the love of cricket and play on the clearing in the woods at every opportunity they get. They call it their very own cricket pitch and feel they own it all for themselves. Sometimes Ed's friends Mark and Fred join them, but they don't love cricket as much as Alex and Ed. This connection eventually makes Ed and Alex very good friends, sharing not just the love of cricket, but comparing and swapping cricket cards and playing with Lego. Spending many afternoons building extravagant and outrageously tall constructions, just to smash them down and rebuild them all over again.

'Oh, wow. Let's do that again Ed,' says Alex excitedly, as he gathers the blocks into a pile with his scooped hands.

Sitting crossed legged under the window, combing her Barbie doll's hair, Aida looks on silently. She would love to join in, but she knows that Ed and Alex don't want her to play with them.

And then, in a flash, Ed and Alex jump over the Lego pieces, dash outside, grab their bikes and disappear in the woods.

Marlene notices that Aida is raring to join them.

'Stay here, Aida. Let them go. You can play with Alex tonight when he gets back,' says Marlene, as she notices the disappointment on Aida's face. 'Why don't you go next door and ask Sandy if you can play with Max for a while?'

And with that, Aida's out in a flash.

It's comforting and important to Marlene and Nick to have good neighbours. Good to be friends, but keep a little distance as well.

'We don't want to be in each other's pockets,' says Marlene to Nick as she dries the dishes.

'What does that mean — in pockets?' asks Alex.

'Well, it means you don't want to be with them all day, every day. It's important we live our lives in our home, but of course, they are welcome to come over for a coffee and chat every now and again,' says Marlene.

'Just like I have Ed come over and play with me?' asks Alex.

'Yes, that's right. But you have to ask before he's allowed.'

'Yes, Mum. I know,' he replies with a frown.

******

Chapter 5

The ten o'clock appointment the following Wednesday at Mount Beauty Primary School confirms the immediate enrolment of Alex in grade one, and the subsequent enrolment of Aida in prep in the new year.

'Nice to meet you all. Please take a seat Mr and Mrs Bennet,' says Mr Angus, as he points to the chairs in front of him.

'Nick and Marlene is fine,' says Nick with a big smile. 'This is Alex and this is Aida. She'll be joining you next year.'

They sit in front of the big wooden desk, clearly displaying a timber nameplate trimmed in brass with 'George Angus, Principal' on it. His desk is covered with stacked trays full to the rim with files, and papers strewn everywhere. He straightens a framed photo of him and his wife, presumably, after he sits down and makes himself comfortable as he nudges his armchair closer to his desk. The seconds of the clock tick-tock loudly behind him as Marlene and Nick patiently wait for him to start the conversation.

'So, you must be Alex?' he finally asks.

Alex nods.

'And you are Aida?'

Aida also nods, as she moves closer to her mum.

'You've recently moved here to Mount Beauty?' he asks, as he looks up at Nick.

'Yes, only a few weeks actually.'

'All settled in, I hope?'

'As much as we can be,' responds Nick, as he turns to Marlene for acknowledgement.

'Very good. Very good. Oh, and here is Miss Potter,' he says, looking up at the young woman entering the room, relieved he doesn't have to continue with small talk.

Alex is very excited to meet his class teacher, a young Miss Potter, who welcomes them all warmly after she closes the heavy door behind her. Wearing thick black-rimmed glasses, a full floral skirt held tight around her waist with a large red belt that matches her lipstick colour, she makes her way behind the desk and stands next to Mr Angus. She carefully goes over the curriculum, and briefly describes the school layout to Alex, who listens intently with big, wide eyes, eager to get started. And so does Aida.

'Any questions?' she asks, as she adjusts her glasses on her nose.

'No, not at all,' says Marlene. 'Well, not for now at least. I'm sure Alex will have plenty when we get home.'

'You will be very happy here, I'm sure,' says Mr Angus, squeezing Alex's shoulder lightly as they stand up and make their way to the door. 'Miss Potter will take you to the office to complete your enrolment and then show you around the school.'

'Oh, I'm sure he will be very happy,' confirms Marlene. 'Thank you, Mr Angus.'

'Thank you, Miss Potter. We'll see you on Monday,' he says, as he warmly shakes Nick's and Marlene's hands goodbye.

The receptionist smiles as Miss Potter does the introductions when they get to the front office desk. Forms are completed and signed, and birth certificates for both Alex and Aida are photocopied.

'Welcome, Alex. I'm sure I'll see you around the schoolyard. And we'll see you next year, Aida. No need for payment for Alex this term, Mr Bennet. There's only a few weeks of school left before we break up for Christmas holidays,' says the receptionist, as she hands them back their certificates.

'Thank you very much,' says Nick.

'And here is the sick bay, Alex. But we hope you won't need it.' Miss Potter laughs as they say goodbye to the receptionist and walk towards the long corridor leading to the classrooms.

'The library is behind the school hall, Alex. I hope you like to read. We have so many lovely books for you to choose from.'

Alex smiles. He does like reading, but he likes cricket best, Marlene would like to say, but she holds back.

With Alex clutching his dad's hand and Aida holding her mum's, they are shown around the school and yard. Aida stands on her tippy toes as she peers through the windows, whilst Alex tries desperately to see Ed in his classroom.

'It looks like a cool school, Alex,' Nick says to his son. 'You will love it here. Well, I've got to go now guys. Got to get to work. See you at home tonight.' Nick pecks a kiss on Marlene's cheek and leaves for the office.

Marlene and the children say goodbye to Miss Potter and they walk to the Newsagent and General Store to buy Alex's school supplies in readiness to start school the following Monday.

Alex can't wait for Ed to come home so he can tell him he's ready for school.

'We can ride to school together, Ed,' he says with a big smile.

Ed is happy too that he has a mate to ride with.

******

Chapter 6

Alex doesn't get much sleep the night before starting at his new school. His mind races in anticipation of meeting and making new friends, but is comforted that Ed will be with him.

Waking early the next morning, proudly sporting a brand-new blue t-shirt and grey shorts, he gulps down his breakfast and is keen to rush out the door. He is happy to see Ed waiting outside his house for him, and after a quick hi they slowly make their way down Edge Street, turning right onto Main Road and then left onto Lakeside Avenue to school.

'It's a dreary old day today,' says Marg, leaning on her fence as she looks up to the sky, when she sees Marlene and Aida. 'I hope it's not going to rain. Very strange for a summer's day out here.'

'They'll be right, Marg. You know what boys are like. A light shower is not going to stop them doing what they want to do. And I have my umbrella, just in case,' Marlene says, giving it a little shake.

And with that, as Marg turns to go back inside the house, Marlene realises that Marg too is pleased that Ed has someone to ride to school with, just as she is with Alex.

But even though Marlene and Aida walk briskly behind them, the boys race ahead and beat them to the school.

Alex is surprised to see his dad waiting by the school gate when they arrive.

'I'm glad you made it,' whispers Marlene in Nick's ear.

'Wouldn't miss it for the world,' Nick whispers back, as he puts his arm around her.

'Alex. Stand next to Ed and I'll take a photo of you both.'

Marlene quickly opens up the umbrella over Nick's head, to protect the camera from the light drizzle that has just started.

With big cheesy grins, and their arms around each other, Alex and Ed smile just as the camera clicks and the flash goes off.

'Have a great day, Alex,' says Nick, as the school bell rings. 'I'll hear all about it tonight, eh, mate?'

'Yeah, Dad,' responds Alex who is keen to get into class.

Miss Potter sits Alex next to Ed. She knows they are friends, and wants to make sure that Alex settles in. After all, there is only a month left of school and she wants him to assimilate quickly.

Ed is keen to show Alex around the yard at playtime. The classmates crowd around him, and he feels part of the school in no time. But he prefers to hang out with Ed. Even though they are the same age, Ed looks considerably older, being so tall and heavy built, and Alex feels protected standing next to him.

'It's a much smaller school than my other one in Beaumaris, Mum, isn't it?' he says to Marlene as she prepares dinner.

'Yes, most country schools are.'

'I've met all the other kids and I think they like me, Mum,' he says with a pensive look on his face. 'It's easy to remember their names because the class is small. And Miss Potter has put me in the Gold team for sports. That's the team that Ed's in, so I'm sure we're going to win all the competitions.'

Marlene laughs. She knows Alex will give it his best shot — he always does.

With only a trickle of young families moving into town, it is noticeable that school enrolments are low. But Marlene prefers it this way.

'He'll get better attention in a small class,' she says to Nick, who has some concerns about the small number of pupils.

'I guess so,' replies Nick, peering over his newspaper at her.

It becomes routine that Alex and Ed ride to and from school together. On their way home, their loud chitter-chatter and laughter is heard as they turn into Edge Street.

'Alex is home,' yells Aida when they appear around the corner.

'See you later, Alex,' yells Ed.

'Yep. See you after dinner, Ed,' answers Alex.

As soon as dinner is finished, Ed and Alex jump on their bikes and rush into the woods, screaming with joy.

'Be home before sunset, Alex,' Marlene manages to yell out before they cross the road.

'So, what do you like best at the new school, Alex?' asks Nick as they snuggle up together on the couch before bedtime.

'I like the playground, Dad.' He jumps up, eyes widening with excitement and hand movements, to help with his expressions.

'It has a cricket pitch. Ed and I play cricket with the other boys at lunchtime, but when the bigger boys get there before us, we play chasey around the schoolyard. I like the library too, Dad, but my other school library was much bigger. Miss May let me choose a book to take home today. I have to bring it back next Tuesday. I'll get it and show you, Dad.'

Nick chuckles with delight that his son is settling in nicely. Alex is such a carefree, accepting and kind soul, and Nick doesn't anticipate any problems.

Unfortunately, there is no kindergarten in Mount Beauty, and Marlene is not keen to drive to Bright for just a few hours a week. So Aida stays home with her mum until she can attend school in the new year.

'She'll be right to start school next year,' Marlene assures Nick. 'After all, she already knows her alphabet and is getting better with her numbers. I'll spend some time with her during the day. She'll be fine, Nick.'

Chapter 7

In the morning, as Aida watches her favourite children's shows, Marlene sings along with her from the kitchen whilst clearing the table and washing up. The children songs are all too familiar to them both, singing them every day after breakfast.

After Marlene finishes her chores, they snuggle on the floor, lean their backs against the couch, and read together. Aida has already gone into the toy box under the coffee table and has chosen her favourite book, *The Monster At The End of This Book*. Marlene giggles, as it's always the same book she chooses.

'Don't you want to pick a different book today, Aida?'

'No,' is her quick response.

In the afternoon they spend time in the garden. The car boot is filled with garden waste, dead branches and an accumulation of broken bricks and concrete lumps found under bushes and around the yard, before they are taken to the tip, just a short drive out of town. Aida likes to help her mum, but prefers to dance around the garden collecting dandelions and placing them in a row on the steps to the back door.

'These are for you, Mummy,' she says when she catch's Marlene's attention.

Marlene smiles and continues with her tasks.

Once the garden is cleared, Marlene's focus is on creating a small vegetable patch; something she has wanted to do for a long time. Every now and again, with crossed arms over her chest, she stops, takes a deep breath and checks her work. She is pleased on how it's all progressing. The look on her face proves how proud she is as the garden starts to take place.

A shallow row of small shrubs, now trimmed, hug the back and side boundaries. The vegetable patch is marked out ready for digging, and the rest of the garden is grassed, not with new, premium lawn, but existing growth, with just enough thickness and bounce for the children to play on. Marlene is confident that the hard work she is putting in will reap rewards in the coming months.

'Mummy, are we getting a swing set, like you promised?' asks Aida.

'Yes, we will, sweetheart. As soon as the garden is finished.'

When the back garden is laid out and planted, her focus shifts to the front garden. Once again making several trips to the tip, she cleans out all the rubbish, slightly trims the hanging rose bushes, and gently turns the soil, hopeful for summer rain to invigorate it. She is quite aware of the harsh summer conditions that Mount Beauty can experience and prepares for these. The Japanese maple, still in its pot, is placed on the east side of the house, in the shade away from the anticipated scorching rays and westerly winds.

'This can be planted next autumn,' she whispers to herself.

The neighbours, now becoming a little more friendly, stop when they see her outside. And it's not just the weather they talk about now; it's the garden.

'You're doing such a great job, Marlene. It's really taking shape and looks beautiful,' says Mrs Robinson over the fence.

'And so does your garden too, Mrs Robinson. The roses look stunning in full bloom. I'll be asking for cuttings in the winter, you know.'

'Of course, dear. I'll get Henry to cut some for you,' she responds.

Everyone that walks past admires the hard work she is putting in to make the house 'a real home' and, with small talk, she learns a little more about the neighbours each time.

She learns that Henry and Joan Robinson are declining in health, hence why they moved from their farm into town. Their children live away in Melbourne and Adelaide, which means that Mrs Robinson has the sole care of her husband.

'They visit when they can, the children, but you know, they are busy with work and it's hard for them to drive up all the time. But we're fine,' she says convincingly.

'Well, yell out if you need help, won't you, Mrs Robinson,' says Marlene.

'Thank you, dear,' she responds, as she slowly makes her way indoors. She knows that Marlene means it and is thankful to know this.

'Mummy, can I play with Max?' asks Aida, when she sees Sandy and Max make their way home.

'Just a little while as I finish cleaning up,' says Marlene.

Aida happily skips off to play with Max under the wooded canopy across the road, in eyesight of both Marlene and Sandy.

'Be careful, you two. Don't go too far into the woods. Stay close to the path where we can see you,' yells Sandy, as she has a quick chat with Marlene.

Sandy is excessively protective of Max; perhaps being a single mum she feels she has to be. Max is very attached to her and she knows he won't venture far from her. Keeping up the conversation with Marlene, Sandy's eyes are locked on Max and Aida.

'She watches him like a hawk,' says Marlene to Nick that night. 'It's too much and over the top.'

'She's obviously scared that something will happen to him. I'm sure you'll know more about the situation once you get to know her better. And she needs to get to know us a little better, too. Give her time, Marlene, give her time.'

'Sandy told me that Max's father's name is also Nick. What a coincidence. Sandy had us over for afternoon tea today, and I saw a photo of him holding Max when he was a baby, and they look so alike. Actually, there were lots of photos of them throughout the house. I guess they are a reminder for Max that he has a father. It's good for Max to see that. It's funny how she never mentions him though. It's so sad he is not with them.'

Nick continues to read the newspaper, and nods in agreement. 'I'm sure she'll tell you more when she's ready.'

With Nick putting in extra hours at the office, he arrives home tired almost every night, but is pleased on how the business is progressing.

'I had Joe from the butcher's come in again today. Such a nice bloke. He wants me to look at his financials. He said he hasn't had anyone look at them in years. Jack's wife Lisa also popped in to introduce herself. Such a lovely lady. Jack and her are such a nice couple. She said she helps Jack out once or twice a week to keep her out of mischief. And the phone calls are picking up, too. Not sure if I'll need an office girl soon. I am managing on my own for now, but will see how things pan out,' he says, as he twitches his nose and adjusts his glasses.

'Once Aida settles into school next year, I can come in for a few hours if you want,' says Marlene. 'That will certainly help you, won't it?'

'Not now, love. We'll see.'

And then Nick turns to the kids, winks at them with a big smile, before they all tumble onto the lounge floor for a tackle and tickles.

'Tickle me, Daddy, tickle me,' they both shout as they laugh.

Marlene's big smile on her face displays true wholesome contentment.

With the summer night wind now calm, and the children fast asleep, Marlene retreats to bed and is nodding off to sleep as Nick slips into bed next to her. He snuggles up and listens to her light breathing, being careful not to disturb her. He turns over and ever so gently puts his arm around her body and closes his eyes. His mind too awake to fall asleep, he mulls over his day's activities, and the tasks ahead of him for the next day, the next week and even into the new year. Oh, how the children have grown so quickly. The years seem to have flown. Life is easy now. Life is happy. And he then slowly drifts off to sleep, with his arm still wrapped around her.

*****

Chapter 8

The afternoon summer sun is hot, but Alex doesn't care. He is far too busy playing cricket with Ed than to worry about the scorching rays on his face.

'You're out,' shouts Ed.

'No, I'm not,' he shouts back.

They continue for a little while, before deciding it is time to go home.

'Gotta go, Ed,' Alex shouts. Fearing his mum's punishment for getting home late, Alex shoves the ball tightly into his trouser pocket, picks his bike up off the ground, sloppily saddles it and makes a dash for home. As he bolts off, he turns around and looks back at Ed, who is now also getting on his bike.

'Bye, Ed. See you tomorrow,' he shouts, as he continues to look back at him.

But, whilst looking back at Ed, he doesn't notice the swerve in the path and crashes into an old tree trunk protruding out in front of him. He falls to the ground, head first, his hand and arm gashed, legs caught in the spikes. He screams in pain.

'Alex! Alex, are you alright?' shouts Ed, as he speeds up to him when he sees him fall.

There is blood all over Alex's hand and face. Ed quickly jumps off his bike and throws it to the ground.

'Are you alright, Alex?' Ed asks again.

Alex groans in pain.

With his arm around Alex's waist, Ed helps him up.

'Can you walk, Alex? Lean on me. I'll help you home,' says Ed.

Clutching his head with one hand and the injured arm bent close to his chest, Alex looks down at his t-shirt and cries louder as he sees blood dripping down from his face.

'Come on, Alex, I'll help you walk,' says Ed, with his hand supporting his back.

Alex bravely limps beside him, scrunching his face in pain. They're not even thinking about their bikes left behind.

'Come on, Alex, we're nearly there,' assures Ed, still supporting him.

'Mrs Bennet!' Ed shouts. 'Mrs Bennet!' he shouts louder, as they get closer to the house.

Ed leans Alex against the fence, as he rushes into the house.

'Mrs Bennet! Alex is hurt.'

Instantly, Marlene drops everything and bolts outside. After inspecting his injuries, she runs back in to get clean towels to wrap around his wounds. She yells, 'Ed, please take Aida home with you. Can you let Nick know I'm taking Alex to the doctor?'

After running into town to let Nick know about the accident, Ed and Aida return to the path to collect the bikes. As they pick up Alex's bike, they notice the front wheel and handlebars are mangled.

'My daddy will buy him a new one,' says Aida.

Ed doesn't respond. He's too worried about Alex's injuries to worry about his bike.

Marlene frantically drives to Alpine Health, where Dr Murphy diagnoses the wounds. The hand and arm are cleaned and bandaged. The legs have no injuries, as they were protected by his jeans. But the right side of Alex's face needs more attention.

'Alex. You'll be fine.' Dr Murphy tries to settle him. 'You're going to have to go to the nearest hospital, Marlene. This cut above the eye needs stitches,' he says, pointing to the deep cut across Alex's eyebrow. 'And the lesion under his eye also needs to be looked at. Bright Hospital is the closest. They will be able to attend to him there immediately. I'll bandage everything up loosely, and give them a call to let them know you're on your way.'

'Thank you, Dr Murphy.' And in a dash, Marlene and Alex are back in the car and on their way to hospital.

The Emergency doctor greets them as they enter through the glass doors. Guiding them into the treatment room, he helps Alex onto the bed.

'Well, Alex. I'm Ben. Let's see what's happened here,' he says reassuringly.

He goes over the injuries, inspecting each one closely, in particular the facial cuts and, even more importantly, the gash under his right eye. After checking his arm, hand and legs, he returns to the facial cuts.

'This can't be stitched unfortunately, Mrs Bennet,' he says as he inspects the skin tear under Alex's eye. 'The skin is too thin. It will heal in time, but I'm afraid as it heals and dries up, the bottom eyelid may be pulled down. Even if we tape it, you can't prevent the tightness of the healing skin. He's lucky he didn't lose his eye, Mrs Bennet. Really lucky.'

On hearing this, Alex sobs a little louder. With Marlene standing behind him with her hands on his shoulders, the doctor continues inspecting Alex's face with his bright torch.

'The right eyebrow has a deep cut and needs a couple of stitches,' he continues. 'And when healed the eyebrow will have a space in the middle of it. That can't be avoided with the stitches going in.'

'That's okay,' responds Marlene. 'It could have been worse, I suppose.'

Ben agrees with her.

Alex cries as his wounds are cleaned.

After inspecting his other eye, Ben turns to his ears and inspects each one closely.

'Everything good here,' he confirms.

He runs his hands over Alex's head. 'To make sure there are no cuts under his hair,' he whispers.

Antiseptic ointment is spread around the eyebrow in preparation for the small procedure.

'Alex. You're going to have to be very brave now. The cream around the cut will soothe it.' And on saying this, he turns his back to Alex to prepare for the stitches.

With Marlene holding Alex's head still, he screams in pain as the doctor puts the stitches in.

'All done,' he says, as he squeezes Alex's arm. 'You're a very brave boy, Alex.'

The look on Marlene's face is worried and tense.

'He's okay, Mrs Bennet. I also suggest we do a CT scan of his head just to make sure there's no head trauma. Can you come in tomorrow? Will you be able to come in at ten? Is that too early for you?'

'No, no. We'll be here at ten.'

'Pick up some Panadol at the pharmacy on your way out, and make sure he takes it to ease the pain. You'll have to keep the head and hand wrapped until it heals, and no school until Dr Murphy says so. We'll see you tomorrow.'

They return home to an anxious Nick and Aida waiting by the front gate. Aida is sad to see Alex hurt, but she's glad to have him home.

'Dinner's on the table,' whispers Nick, as he greets Marlene. He picks Alex up and carries him inside. Alex flops himself carefully against his dad, still quietly sobbing.

'Wash your hands, Aida. Please help her, Nick,' says Marlene as she settles Alex on the couch in the lounge room.

Nick can see the distressed look on Aida's face, so he playfully throws her over his shoulder, swings her around and carries her to the sink to wash her hands.

The evening is sombre and Alex is comforted by both his mum and dad, with Aida offering as much help as Alex will allow. She pulls the toy box from under the coffee table, to choose a toy for him, but Alex is in no mood to play.

'Not too close, Aida. Alex needs his space,' says Marlene, raising her hand around Alex's face to protect him.

Poor little Aida moves away, almost in tears herself.

Marg and Ed visit.

'He's doing okay, Marg. It'll take time now to heal.'

Ed stands back at first, and then goes up to Alex with pitiful eyes, almost feeling as much pain as Alex is feeling. Not knowing what to say, he blurts out, 'We've put your bike in the shed, Alex.'

Alex nods and gives him a little smile.

'Rest up, Alex,' says Marg, as she gently rubs his arm. 'We'll visit again tomorrow.'

'It's healing nicely,' says Dr Murphy, as he inspects and changes the bandages the following week. 'The CT scan results are all clear. I can say you can go back to school tomorrow, but you'll need to be very careful.'

'Can I play cricket with Ed now?' asks Alex.

'No, not quite yet, young man. You will have to be careful your face doesn't get hit by the ball or, even worse, you don't fall down again. I've bandaged it up tight, so you should be alright. Don't ride your bike until it's totally healed, Alex,' reaffirms Dr Murphy. 'I'd like to see you again next week.'

Alex is not happy that he can't ride his bike, but Ed agrees not to ride his either, until Alex can ride his new bike, too. That makes Alex smile. And for the following week, they walk to school.

At lunchtime, Alex sits by the sidelines, watching Ed play cricket with the other boys, and wishes he was playing too.

'Come on, Ed,' he encourages, when it's Ed's turn to bat.

The next visit to Dr Murphy finds improved healing in the hand and arm, but the gash around his eye and the cut across the eyebrow are still healing. The stitches in the eyebrow are removed and so is the bandage.

'There you go, Alex. Stitches are out now. Keep it clean, Marlene. I'll see you again in two weeks, Alex. Take care of yourself,' says Dr Murphy.

After a warm handshake, they are out the door, happy that the stitches are out and that everything is healing as expected.

******

Chapter 9

Sitting around the kitchen table eating together, Aida says, 'Daddy, Mummy said I can have Max over for my birthday party next week. I'm going to be five. And Sandy said she will bring the cake. A fairy cake with five candles on it.' Aida's big bright eyes light up with excitement.

'That's wonderful, Aida. It will be very special to celebrate your birthday in our new home. It will be great to have Max and Sandy come and watch you blow out your candles. Mummy and Daddy have got you a special present, but you'll have to wait for us to give it to you next week on your birthday.'

'Is it a swing set? Is it? Is it, Daddy?'

Both Marlene and Nick laugh as they turn to look at each other.

'And we need to get you a new dress, Aida,' says Marlene. 'We'll go into town tomorrow and see what we can find. Something special for a big girl.'

'I can't wait, Daddy. It's going to be fun,' she says, jumping up and down on the spot, clapping her hands.

As Alex plays with his food around the plate, he is deep in thought.

'Dad. How can I beat Ed in cricket? I know he's bigger than me, but I can run faster, and he bowls me out before I get a chance to run. I want to bowl him out too.'

With a big smile on his face, Nick's eyes dart up at Marlene, then he pauses and responds, 'Well, son, you may want to learn how to spin. It's not easy and will need lots of practice. Now, I'm not a cricketer, but I have read about the finger and wrist spin. Why don't you and I have a go after we've finished our dinner?'

This is a great incentive for Alex to get stuck into his food and finish everything on his plate. He wastes no time in wiping his mouth with the back of his hand and rushes out the back door.

'Me too,' says Aida, 'I want to play too.'

'You're a girl. You can't play cricket,' Alex yells back.

With Marlene clearing the table and Aida watching them from the back steps, Nick and Alex spend the evening practising.

'Like this, son. Keep your fingers tight around the ball, and twist your wrist just before throwing it. Be careful you don't hurt your injured hand.'

Alex watches closely. So full of confidence, he knows he can do this!

With his tiny hand wrapped around the ball and his dad keeping a close watch, Alex practises throw after throw as Nick rolls the ball on the grass back to him.

'Just keep practising, Alex. You'll get there! And keep your eye on the ball,' says Nick, as he catches it and rolls it back.

The night is warm with a slight breeze, typical of summer in the north east of Victoria. Marlene dries the last of the dishes, and reflects on how blessed they are to have found such an idyllic place and how truly content she is now that they have settled in. Dreams of a happy and healthy future float in and around her head.

She wipes her hands on the tea towel, takes off her apron, hangs it behind the kitchen door, and makes her way to the steps. She sits next to Aida, and is heartened to see Nick and Alex practising their bowling. With her chin up and eyes closed, she breathes deep into the air, then snuggles Aida up to her and puts her face close to hers.

'One, two, three ... ' Marlene's finger runs over Aida's nose.

'Are you counting my freckles, Mummy?'

'Yes, I am. There's a new one on your nose today,' Marlene says.

They both laugh loudly.

Alex turns his head to look at her. Now more than ever he so wants to make his mum proud when he bowls Ed out. Dad too. He wants his dad to be proud, too.

'Look, Mum. Look!' he shouts.

'Be careful, Nick. You don't want the ball to hit his face,' Marlene cautiously warns.

'It's okay, Mum' says Alex, not wanting his dad to stop playing.

Bored and restless, Aida gets up and starts dancing around the garden. In and out of the bushes, her summer dress twirling as she spins on her tippy toes, falling when her feet get stuck in the knotted grass. But with a quiet hum, she picks herself up and continues. Her golden-brown locks fall onto her shoulders before bouncing back up again. With her little hand pushing them away from her face, she continues dancing.

'Look at me, Mummy,' she yells, in her little squeaky voice.

'Beautiful, Aida, just beautiful.'

Aida runs into her mother's arms and squeezes her tight.

Every cheer from Nick to Alex is followed by another loud cheer and a clap from Marlene and Aida, both beaming with joy.

As the sun sets, and they pack up to go inside, Marlene stares at Nick and then at Alex, shakes her head and says, 'Twins, that's what you two are. Twins!'

Her usual long, loving stare at Nick is her silent validation of her love for him; one they're both familiar with, and frequently displayed throughout their ten years of marriage.

'Do I really, really look like Dad, Mum?' Alex asks with a big grin as he makes his way inside.

Her giggles make him happy to look like his daddy. Same thick mop of dark hair, roundish face, same body shape and their very own unique laugh. Marlene thinks it's hilarious when they laugh together, sometimes tickling him on purpose, just to hear him laugh.

As he makes his way to the steps, Nick leans down to kiss Marlene's head and with his arm around her they head in just as it's getting dark.

Teeth brushed, pyjamas on, Alex excitedly races up the stairs, practising his overarm spins.

'Don't run. Be careful,' shouts Marlene as she pokes her head through the kitchen door.

Sitting on the side of his bed, Marlene inspects Alex's face, gently smoothing antiseptic cream over the bottom of his eye and the scab across his eyebrow.

'It's healing nicely, Alex, but I'm afraid you'll have a scar, young man, just like Dr Murphy suspected.'

She inspects the shiny, delicate, white skin forming around the bottom of his eye, quite a contrast to his tanned complexion. She worries that the skin will set tight and the bottom eyelid will be pulled down. The ointment she lightly spreads around the eye may soothe it, but it won't stop the pulling of the eyelid.

'You are very lucky you didn't do more damage. You'll have to be more careful on your bike, Alex, especially in the woods. Slow down when you're riding and watch where you're going,' she says in a stern voice.

'Yes Mum.'

'Night, Alexi,' yells Aida, her usual, night-time ritual from her room.

'Night, Aidie,' he yells back, as he snuggles up to Flops, his bed-time teddy bear, next to him on his pillow.

Aida has always called him Alexi and Alex has called her Aidie since she was baby. These names have stuck and both of them think it's special to have nicknames for each other.

But Alex finds it hard to fall asleep, as his mind conjures up scenarios of spins and twists, hoping to surprise Ed with his new tricks that his dad has shown him and finally bowl Ed out. He can't wait for Dr Murphy to say he can play cricket again. He tosses and turns before finally crashing deep into solid sleep as the wind dies down for the night.

******

Chapter 10

'Come in for a coffee, Marlene,' shouts Sandy from her porch when she sees Marlene and the kids in the front yard the next day.

The children play outside, whilst Sandy and Marlene sit under the verandah sipping iced tea.

'Be careful, Alex,' yells Marlene.

'How is Alex? Are his wounds getting better?' asks Sandy.

'Slowly. He's getting there,' replies Marlene, still keeping a close eye on him.

'And you've finished unpacking? All settled in now?' asks Sandy.

'We seem to have settled in. There are still some boxes we need to empty, but they can wait.'

'Do you miss the city at all?'

'We certainly don't regret the move, Sandy, and we certainly don't miss the city. The overcrowding suburbs, more so now with young families settling out of the city centre. You know, with expansions of new estates going up everywhere, the landscape is changing so much. It's terrible. Backyards have shrunk and apartment buildings are going up everywhere and we feared the children playing outside with so much traffic on the roads. It's not the life we wanted for our children. And you, Sandy? Are you happy here?'

'Sure am,' she replies, as she gets up to take the empty cups into the kitchen. 'I don't ever want to move from here. It's home for us now.'

'Have you noticed tourists starting to trickle in?' asks Sandy when she returns with a box of chocolates to share.

'Yes, I have.' Marlene laughs. 'Just like Nick and I used to do when we would come down for our holiday.'

With the school holidays fast approaching, the locals get ready to bunker down and absorb the swarm of city invaders seeking a mountain and High Country escape. The General Store is busy with bike rentals and camping gear sales, and the other stores stock up with holiday and Christmas supplies. Store owners are pleased that tourists will bring in much needed sales. The 'crazy' season, as they call it, is well and truly awaited and appreciated.

'Dad?' asks Alex. 'Can we go to Kiewa River for a swim on the weekend? Some of the boys in class said they will be going and I think Ed said he is too.'

'There will be plenty of opportunities for us to go, son. Perhaps not this weekend, as I still have so much work to do in the office. Let's wait for the school holidays before we make any plans, eh?'

The television commercials for holiday accommodation and activities are constant. With only a few weeks of school left, Alex and Aida dream of all the adventures they too will be having during the Christmas break. As they lie on their tummies, watching every exciting activity being transmitted to them, they plan their adventures, whilst Marlene and Nick retreat to the porch and enjoy a cold drink whilst chatting over their day.

******

Chapter 11

The loud commotion from downstairs wakes him. There's shouting coming from the kitchen. His mum is screaming and his dad is yelling. There are other voices too, also loud. He sits on the edge of his bed and listens more attentively, but can't make out what they are saying or who else is downstairs. Everyone is yelling over each other. Rubbing his eyes, he grabs Flops by the ears and slowly makes his way down the stairs, being careful not to trip on his long pyjama pants.

All heads turn and look at Alex as he reaches the last step. He can see his dad standing in between two tall, heavy men. One of the men is holding his dad's hands behind his back.

His dad's eyes open wide in fear as he sees Alex. The other man, standing behind the kitchen table, is startled when he too sees him, and fidgets as if he doesn't know what to do next. Nick tries to wriggle free. He looks at Alex and then looks left and right at the men holding him. Alex's eyes dart from his mum to his dad back to his mum, who is clutching Aida tightly.

Surprised and panicked, Marlene yells for him to go back upstairs, as does Nick, but he's confused and doesn't know what to do.

'Alex. Run back upstairs. Alex! Do as you're told. Now, Alex! GO!' Marlene's voice quivers.

But instead of doing as she asks, he runs to her and clings to her leg. He is scared. She puts her arm around him. Her other arm holds Aida, who has now housed her head in Marlene's neck. Alex can feel his mum's body shaking.

'Yuri, please let my family go. Please! Yuri. Viktor. Please let them go. I will do whatever you want,' pleads Nick.

But it seems hopeless. They are not listening.

'You didn't say there were two. Two!' Viktor angrily yells to Yuri. With brow sweating and body still nervously fidgeting, he continues. 'There's only meant to be one.'

As Nick struggles to free himself, Viktor turns to Marlene, walks up to her and screams, 'Which one? Which one? Choose! Which one? Choose. NOW!'

What is he asking her to choose? Marlene is confused and frightened with what Viktor is asking her.

'Choose.' He continues in a thick Russian accent. 'Choose! Choose! Who do you choose — your son or your daughter?' he shouts. He repeats this over and over.

In her confusion Marlene holds Aida and Alex tighter.

Surely he is not asking her which child to choose? Is that what he's asking?

Shaking her head, she pleads pitifully. 'No. No. Please. No.'

He moves closer to her with his nose almost touching hers. She turns her head away from his and squeezes her children tighter. She can smell his anger and she fears for their lives. Everything is happening so fast she can't even think or imagine what he's asking of her.

In an instant, Viktor grabs Alex by the arm. With his other hand he grabs Marlene's chin, squeezing it hard, and whispers angrily in her ear before banging her heavily against the wall.

'Choose, I said.'

Marlene trembles in pain.

This enrages Nick, who vigorously wriggles to try to free himself. But Yuri has a tight hold of both his hands secured behind his back.

'Keep still, Nikolai,' yells Yuri angrily.

Marlene sobs uncontrollably as she tries to hang onto Alex, but Viktor yanks him away from her and she feels him slip away from her grip. She stretches her hand to grab him and as Aida turns around to see what is happening, Marlene's hand instinctually retracts to balance her. Then suddenly, Viktor secures Alex in his hold and walks backwards away from her.

Alex frets and starts crying. Marlene starts to walk towards Viktor, still holding Aida close to her. She stops immediately as she sees Viktor reach under his jacket, into his belt and pull out a gun. She gasps and freezes.

Nick is frenzied. Still struggling to free himself, he bites Yuri on the arm and, painfully, Yuri lets go of him. Nick takes this opportunity to push Yuri away, so that he can get to Alex, but as he does he loses his balance. He attempts to regain his footing and then ....

BANG!

The noise is so loud Marlene's ears feel like they have exploded and her eyes snap shut. Her whole body cringes. She lets out a loud, continuous, piercing scream and doesn't stop. Crying, Aida holds tighter onto her mother's neck. Viktor and Yuri scramble out the kitchen door with Alex.

Marlene looks down. Nick is on the floor. He's not moving. His head is flung to one side and his hands are limp next to him.

She dashes out the front door. The engine of a car and screeching tyres pierces the night. The car sways left to right and the tyres spin as they try to grab the road. Finally gaining traction, with dust and pebbles hurling into the air, the car speeds off.

She screams and keeps screaming as they disappear down Edge Street, taking a sharp left onto Western Highway. Apart from her screams, there's now just silence and darkness.

They're gone! She lets out another long scream. With Aida still in her arms, in a panic, she runs to the end of the street.

'ALEX! ALEX!' she yells.

Holding Aida tighter than ever she looks left, right and then left again, but they're gone.

'Help! Help!' she screams. 'HELP!'

She rushes back to Nick as she turns Aida's head into her neck to cover her eyes. A trickle of blood is gathering under his back. She's trembling in fear and doesn't know what to do. Sobbing, she calls out to him.

'Nick. Nick. Wake up. Dear God, please wake up.'

She puts Aida down so she can free her hands. With one hand under his head and the other gently shaking his chest, she begs, 'Please, Nick, wake up. Wake up. Nick!'

She gets up, clumsily jumps over Aida and stumbles to the phone to dial 000.

'He's been shot. Seven Edge Street,' she shouts. 'They've taken my Alex. Seven Edge Street. HURRY!'

In her confused state, she doesn't hang up. Leaving the phone dangling on its cord against the wall, she runs back outside.

'Help! Please. Help!' she yells.

Sandy has already heard her screams and is rushing to the house. Other neighbours who also hear her cries rush up.

'They've taken my Alex. They've taken my Alex,' yells Marlene in a frenzied stammer. She pushes Sandy away from her and runs down the road screaming.

'Alex! Alex!'

Aida is staring at her father lying on the floor. With Marlene rushing back inside, all Aida can hear are her mother's loud screams and sobs as she repeats Nick's name over and over.

Sandy, Wayne and Marg have made their way to the kitchen. Mrs Robinson is also clumsily staggering in. Ed, who was woken by the commotion, is outside, too frightened to go inside the house.

Aida looks at her mother, confused and scared. Too young to fully understand what is happening, her little body shakes in fear.

'He's been shot. They've taken Alex. They've taken my Alex.' Marlene looks up at her neighbours.

'Quick, Marg. Call the ambulance,' yells Wayne.

In a flash, Marg dashes to the phone.

Wayne kneels down near Nick hoping for some sign of life. He rushes outside. Looks left and right down the street, but there is no one there. He sees Ed, frozen next to the letterbox.

'Ed. Go home, son.'

All the pandemonium is too much for Ed. Wayne pushes past him and races back into the house.

Sandy has her arms around Marlene trying to lift her off Nick. But Marlene isn't budging, so Sandy picks up Aida, cradles her head and wraps her little body around hers. She then puts her down on the couch and sits beside her, glancing at everyone in the kitchen hovering over Nick.

Marlene gets up again, pushes heavily on the fly-wire door and runs back to the road, frantic, not knowing what to do.

She doesn't see Ed still standing there in fear.

'Alex! Alex!' she screams. 'ALEX!'

Returning back to Nick she sits on her heels staring at him. With Marg's arms around her, and as realisation sets in, she rocks back and forth as she hears the ambulance and police sirens approach in the distance.

******

Chapter 12

They say Aida was too young to fully absorb and comprehend everything that happened that night, but she wasn't. Five years old is not too young to know horrors. And the horrors didn't stop that night.

The ambulance and police arrive. They cordon off the street with police tape and police cars. Their blue and red flashing lights illuminate the street like it's Christmas. Sirens belt out a piercing sound that is heard for miles around town and beyond. After a quick brief from Marlene and the neighbours, police motorbikes screech down Edge Street and onto Western Highway. Police cars do the same.

The police take over the house. On the advice of Detective Blyth, Sandy offers Marlene and Aida to go to her house for the night, but Marlene is insistent on staying home.

Aida tries to keep her eyes open, but eventually falls asleep in Sandy's arms.

She sees the police are still there when she wakes in her bed during the early hours of the morning. She slowly gets up, walks to the landing and peers through the stair rails, watching everyone rushing around in a flurry. She sees Max asleep on the couch with a blanket over him, and Sandy has her arms around Marlene, who is sitting on the edge of the armchair crying. Two men wheel a long stretcher, carrying something covered in a black plastic sheet. She's too scared to contemplate what it may be and dismisses that thought instantly. She silently retreats back to her bedroom, too frightened to make her way to her mum and too frightened to fall asleep. She clutches her soft doll close to her and pulls the sheet over her head.

With the sun streaming in, and the wind blowing softy against the curtains, Aida wakes and sits on the edge of her bed. She listens, before venturing quietly downstairs. Sandy and Max are not there, and neither are the other neighbours. It is just her and her mum and a house full of people, busy about the place, so busy they don't even notice her.

She finds her mother in the lounge, still sitting precariously on the edge of the armchair, gently rocking. Her head is down, held up by her hand, and with her other hand soaks up tears in a sodden tissue.

Aida sneaks up to her and Marlene picks her up and squeezes her into her chest, rocking her back and forth.

The kitchen has tape across the doorway and people in white jumpsuits, masks and blue plastic gloves swarm in and out and all around.

Carrying big heavy bags, the police search through every room meticulously. When they lay the bags on the floor and flip the lid open, Aida can see instruments, tape, plastics bags, swabs, notebooks, and lots of other things that Aida doesn't understand what they may be used for.

'They look scary, Mum, all these people,' says Aida, wrapping her arms around Marlene's neck. But she knows they aren't.

'They are doing a special job, Aida, and are helping us.' She's not expecting a reply from Aida.

Sandy pops in.

'Do you want me to take Aida, Marlene? I can give her breakfast and she can play with Max. Here is a sandwich and coffee for you. Do you want to come too? Stay at our house for a while? Get some rest?'

'No, I'm alright, Sandy. Thank you. That would be good if you can take Aida,' she replies in a whisper.

Aida is glad to go next door and have breakfast with Max, but she doesn't want to leave her mum. As Sandy grabs Aida's little hand, they go up to her room, and Sandy helps her change out of her pyjamas.

'Mummy said I can wear my new dress for my birthday today,' she says to Sandy.

'Okay, sweetheart. You can wear whatever you like,' says Sandy, with tears in her eyes, as she helps her put her arms through the dress.

As they head for the front door, Aida turns round to look at her mum, but Marlene is not looking at her. She still has her head down, wiping away more tears.

Aida doesn't like all those people in her home. She is waiting for Sandy to bring out her birthday cake. She wants everyone to sing her happy birthday and desperately wants to open the present from her mum and her dad.

'Will I blow out my candles later?' she asks Sandy after she's finished her breakfast.

'Best we check with your mum first,' responds Sandy.

She waits for Sandy to wish her a happy birthday, but she doesn't. She waits all day. Aida doesn't mention it again, sensing that it's not the right thing to ask right now. There is no cake or celebration. She thinks that maybe later in the day her mum, dad and Alex will remember, and she'll have her party. But they don't. No one remembers. Not even her mum, who is still crying at home.

'Sandy, can I go home now?' asks Aida. She has finished her lunch and is anxious to get back home to be with her mum.

'Not now, love,' Sandy whispers. 'Best you wait for Mummy to come and get you. I'm sure she'll be here soon. Why don't you and Max watch a bit of TV?'

They snuggle up on the carpet, munch on biscuits from the saucer next to them and are soon captivated in the world of children's entertainment. And when Sandy comes in to check on them they are both sound asleep. It seems the lack of sleep the night before has caught up with them, and Sandy is thankful they are both resting, so that she too can have a quick nap.

In no time, television, radio and newspaper crews arrive. They swarm the house and surrounding area like ravenous ants, eager to penetrate the police blocks. Vans and station wagons with roof platforms hold huge, heavy camera units, and camera tripods are parked along the footpath, spilling out onto the dirt road. Frenzied reporters itch to catch the latest, to make the 'breaking' news of the day and the headlines for the evening news. Marlene is annoyed to see them, but grateful that police can hold them back and finally, after a short, sharp update from Detective Blyth, they are coerced away, but as expected, return later in the day and the days that follow, just as eager and just as hungry.

'Go away. Go away!' With her hands covering her ears, Marlene cries to them in frustration from her kitchen window.

******

Chapter 13

The police continue their investigation the next day, and many days after that. They look at everything. Aida can't understand why they want to look at her dolls and all the stuff in her room. But she thinks it is good of them to put everything back in their place once they have finished.

They spend a lot of time in Alex's room and she sees them put some of Alex's clothes in brown paper bags. They even go to her mum and dad's room and do the same with some of her dad's things. Then they go to the storeroom and open up boxes that her mum and dad haven't had time to open yet. They take everything out, look at it and then put some of it back in the boxes and other things in their bags.

They use long measuring tapes, and take lots of photos. They look closely at things with a special light that makes invisible things visible. Aida wishes she had one of those lights. They collect anything they find of interest into their paper bags, scribble something on the white label and then put them into bigger bags and take them to the police van parked outside.

The furniture, doors, door handles and walls are lightly dusted with white stuff. Aida thinks this is very amusing, but they all have very serious looks on their faces, especially when they get so close that their noses almost touch the doorknob. She also thinks it's very funny how they speak softly amongst themselves and then speak loudly over the police walkie-talkies. Soft, loud. Soft, loud.

There are even police outside looking behind Marlene's bushes and on the grass. She is so glad they don't see Alex's cricket ball on the bottom step, hiding behind the weeds. When they're not looking, Aida sneaks out, picks it up and takes it upstairs and hides it in her room so she can give it back to Alex when he comes home. She doesn't want the police to put it in their brown paper bags and take it away.

After hiding Alex's ball, she makes her way down the stairs to the landing. She sits on her knees, holds on to the stair rails, and looks at the lady with her arm around her mum's shoulders. She guesses that the lady's arm must be heavy, because Marlene pushes it away, still sobbing and still trembling. The nice lady looks up, sees Aida and makes her way to her. Ever so gently, she entices her to come down the stairs.

'Would you like a glass of milk, Aida?' she asks.

Aida shakes her head.

'Mummy is a bit upset,' she continues. 'Those men frightened her. Did you see them?' asks Constable Dawn.

Aida nods yes.

'Can you remember their faces, Aida?'

'No,' is Aida's quiet response.

She asks her questions of that horrible night. But Aida can't remember much. All she can remember is lots of shouting and then a big bang. She can remember seeing her dad on the floor, but she doesn't know what's happened to Alex.

'It was my birthday yesterday,' she says to the constable. 'Sandy has my fairy cake and we are going to celebrate tonight when Daddy and Alex come home.'

With tears welling in her eyes, Constable Dawn looks down to the floor.

'Why don't we celebrate your birthday another day, Aida, once the police have finished their job? Won't that be good? Do you think you can wait till then?'

Aida nods. She's not quite sure if she is happy with that, but it sounds like a good idea to have her daddy and brother here.

'Leave her alone,' shouts Marlene as she rushes into the hallway in a fury. She grabs Aida and squeezes her tight against her.

'Just find Alex will you,' she snaps at the constable.

Detective Blyth and the Bush Search and Rescue team organise and despatch search parties, including the fire brigade and many local volunteers and neighbours that have gathered in front of the house. Marlene can hear the loud instructions as Detective Blyth and the Fire Chief distribute maps and point the groups in different directions. Some disperse down the street toward town, others make their way to the highway and another group heads into the woods.

Nail-biting anxiety and lack of sleep has crippled Marlene as she paces around the house, intermittently looking through the windows for any sign that Alex is found. The stress and pressure is profound.

They ask Marlene for the keys to the office and the same intense search is done there. Police go through paperwork, files, Nick's appointment book and take some of his clothing.

Police questioning is continuous. At times, Marlene gets upset that she can't remember all the details they are asking and raises her voice and hands in frustration. They want to know everything: times, people's names and what they looked like. She tells them their names, which the police say is 'a good start', but she can't remember much more than that.

'Yuri and Viktor,' she keeps repeating. 'That's what Nick called them. Yuri and Viktor.'

'So, he knew them?'

'I don't know. He never spoke about his clients. I don't know. I have never seen them before. He has never mentioned them,' she repeats over and over.

'Marlene, Nick's appointment book shows he met with them last week. Did you know that? He has a pencilled appointment with Viktor last Wednesday.'

'No. He didn't say. He doesn't talk about his appointments with me.'

******

Chapter 14

It isn't the same playing with her dolls in her room. Aida feels alone, even though the house is full of people. Marlene constantly calls out to her, wanting to know where she is. Aida is sad. She is not allowed to go outside anymore, not even the back yard. When Sandy is not working, she can go next door and play with Max, but she just wants her life to be like it was before. She wants Alex and her dad to come back so that she can blow out the candles on her cake and she wants to open her birthday present. She wants to see Alex beat Ed in cricket. She wants Alex to make them proud like he dreamed. She longs to hear Alex and her dad laugh so that Marlene can be happy again. And she waits for Alex to wish her goodnight like he always does.

'Night, Aidie. Night, Alexi,' she whispers to herself.

And she wants her daddy back.

Aida doesn't sleep in her bed after that night and not for a long time after that. She is scared to sleep on her own and Marlene wants her close. She sleeps in her mum's big bed, snuggled close to her.

From the bedroom window, Aida can see Ed come around with stumps under his arm, hoping Alex has come back, and he is saddened when Aida shakes her head. He turns away, head bowed and heads for the clearing.

He stops coming to the front door after a while, but Aida sees him ride his bike and when he comes close to the house, he slows down, perhaps hoping to get a glimpse of Alex, wishing him back. And that's when she starts to understand that it's not just her mum and her that are hurting; so is Ed and perhaps all Alex's other friends too. She starts to wonder why it's taking so long for Alex to come back home.

Some of her mum's and dad's friends from the city come and visit, but they don't stay long, because Marlene is not in the mood to entertain or talk with them. They stay just a short while, and then leave, with sad looks on their faces. Neighbours visit, bring home-cooked meals, put them on the kitchen table, give Marlene and Aida a hug and then also leave. Joe the butcher comes and puts a meat tray in the fridge. 'For later,' he says to Marlene.

Jim from the General Store visits with his wife Angie. They sit nervously in the lounge asking, 'Is there anything we can do, Marlene?'

But Marlene just shakes her head side to side with a quiet, 'No, thank you'.

Jack and his wife Lisa talk quietly to Detective Blyth in the corner of the hallway under the stairs. Jack listens intently and Lisa gently dries tears from her eyes. They whisper for a long time, with Jack answering lots of questions that Detective Blyth is asking him, and then shake hands. Jack and Lisa go into the lounge room to give Marlene a hug and another to Aida before they also quietly leave.

'Let us know if you need anything, Marlene,' whispers Lisa.

Sandy comes over after every work day and every other day too. She pops a warm meat pie on the table, and bread rolls in the bread box, and asks Marlene if there's anything she can help with before taking Aida home with her to play with Max. Marlene understands that it's not Max that wants Aida to play with him, but it's Sandy's way of getting Aida out of the house, and give Marlene quiet time on her own.

During the days when Sandy is at work, Aida retreats to her bedroom and plays with her Barbies, talking to them as if they were real people. She pretends that Ken is her daddy, lifting him up above her shoulders and twirling him around.

******

Chapter 15

A few days later, distracted by the door bell, Aida throws down her dolls and rushes down the stairs almost tripping over her feet as the door flings open. It isn't her dad or Alex as she hoped, but it's the next best thing.

'Grandma! Mummy, Grandma's here!' she shouts and jumps into her grandma's arms.

Aida can tell by the size of her bag that this time Edna plans to stay longer and this puts a smile on Aida's face.

'Grandpa can't come because he is not well,' Edna says to Aida, whilst side glancing at Marlene.

A glance back and a nod is all Marlene can muster initially, then she slowly makes the effort to get off the couch to give her mother a hug.

Aida shows Edna upstairs to the spare room and helps her settle in.

'Look, Grandma. This is a new wardrobe to put all your things in. Daddy bought it at Jim's up the street.'

'Thanks, dear. This room is very nice. Let's open the window to get some fresh air in.'

And with that she puts her bag down on the trunk and slides up the window. At last, Aida has someone to play with and someone to talk to now. Holding hands, they make their way downstairs.

With a long sigh, Edna gives her daughter another hug, a long lasting one as Marlene flops her head on her mother's shoulder.

In a trance, Marlene releases the hug and walks to the bench, trying hard to hide her quite sobs. She makes two cups of tea and gives Aida a cup of milk. Chairs are pulled loosely to the kitchen table, and with heads down and Aida sitting on grandma's lap, they silently take a sip.

Marlene knows all too well why Edna is here. Edna has sensed the desperation during the daily phone calls to her, and is concerned for her wellbeing and also Aida's. Even though she did not want to leave Bill back home alone, Edna felt she was needed here more. And she is.

Marlene is not coping. Her worry for Alex is relentless and Nick's murder is incomprehensible. Why? No one seems to be able to answer this one question.

And choose. Choose what? Who? Did she really have to choose between Alex and Aida? Is that what Viktor was asking of her?

Edna takes over the daily chores, plays with Aida and keeps a 'silent' supervision of Marlene. Even though counselling has been offered, Marlene has refused it.

'I'm fine, Mum. I don't want people coming and going in and around the house any more. I'll be better once they find Alex.'

Edna is certainly not convinced that her daughter is fine. Marlene spends most of the time lying down, has very little to eat and cries a lot. She rings Detective Blyth every day, sometimes twice a day. Late afternoons, she leaves the house to look up and down the street, walks up to the highway, stares left to right and then makes her way back home, sometimes walking through the woods and stopping at the clearing, staying there for hours and hours. She hangs onto every hope when Detective Blyth rings to say he is visiting, and each time her hopes are crushed when there are no new updates.

Aida, in desperate need of Marlene's attention, now turns to Edna for support. Edna is thankful that Aida has Max to play with.

'She needs all the distraction she can get for now,' Edna says to Marlene.

When Aida sees Ed head off to the cricket pitch, she follows him, and sits by the sidelines watching him and his friends play. She wishes that Alex was playing too.

Ed doesn't say anything. He understands why she's there. He just throws a glance at her every now and again and she's happy.

When the game's over, she follows the boys out of the clearing, through the path and crosses the road home.

'Bye, Ed' she says.

Without a word, he waves back to her, before making a quick dash home.

******

Chapter 16

'That's the doorbell,' says Edna. 'It's the police.'

'What do they want now?' asks Marlene, as she heads to open the door.

'May we come in?' Detective Blyth says.

'Yes, certainly. Come in,' says Marlene.

Her heart flutters with hope they may have news on Alex. But the look on the faces of Detective Blyth's and his young colleague doesn't seem to bear good news.

Her hands twitch as she leads the way into the lounge room.

Edna wipes her hands on the tea towel, throws it on the kitchen bench, and follows them. She also has hope to hear some good news. But it's not good news.

'There has been a break-in. We were called to Nick's business. The office has been ransacked.'

'Oh,' gasps Marlene, as both her hands rush to the mouth.

'It appears that whoever broke in must've been looking for something. The back door was jimmied open, and the office and storeroom ransacked. Our inspectors are there now. Would you be able to come and have a look, Marlene? We really need your help to ascertain if anything has been taken.'

'Uh! Do you think it's the same people? Do you know if this is all related? Are they locals? They must still be here then. They must be! They still have Alex?' Marlene demands, standing up from the couch.

'We don't have any answers yet, Marlene, but we are looking at every scenario.'

'Mum, can you look after Aida whilst I go into town?'

'You go, dear. We'll be fine,' replies Edna, as she pulls Aida into her.

Pinning her hair behind her ears, and patting down her dress, Marlene takes a deep breath, grabs her bag and keys and follows them out the door.

Edna peeps through the kitchen window as Aida jumps onto the bench to also have a look.

There are police cars at the front of the office, and also in the laneway at the back, carrying paper bags into their van, whilst other officers are going about their job inside. A few spectators hang about, talking quietly amongst themselves, and some are being questioned by police officers scribbling down notes in their little notebooks.

It is a shock to see Nick's office in this state. After all the work he had put into it, now it looks like a rubbish heap. The back door almost taken off its hinges. Papers and files strewn everywhere. The desk drawers pulled out, and Nick's chair thrown onto its back. The filing cabinets emptied and papers spilling into the hallway. Police officers take fingerprints off doorknobs, walls, cabinets and desks.

Marlene is in shock. Just like they did at her home a few days back, their presence and actions are all too familiar. She certainly didn't expect this. She hadn't been to the office since that horrible night. It hadn't even crossed her mind to go there.

She carefully and cautiously treads from the back area, through the hallway, taking a quick look in Nick's office, and then steps into the reception area. She initially thinks they haven't taken anything from the front room, but as she looks up at the wall above the front desk, she notices the frame missing. She glances around the floor, sees the smashed glass on the ground and the business registration certificate missing from its frame. That's all she can tell that has been taken. She can't believe this has happened.

'It seems they were in a hurry. It also appears they may have been looking for something. They didn't bother too much in the front room, so based on the mess in Nick's office whatever they were looking for must've been in there, in his files. Can you think of anything that Nick might've had that they were looking for?' asks Detective Blyth.

'I wouldn't have a clue. I left Nick's business up to him. I never asked him about his clients, and he never spoke of them. What could they possibly want? Are they the same people that murdered him? The same people that have taken my Alex? Are they? Are they, you think? Oh, and by the way, Nick's business certificate that was hanging above the desk is missing. Have you got it? Or have they taken it?'

'We don't have it, Marlene. It's possible they have taken it. Is there anything else you can see that is missing?'

'I don't think so. I'm not sure with all this mess in the way,' responds Marlene. 'Do you think it's Yuri and Viktor that broke in?'

'We need to ascertain when this happened and then obviously by whom. We can't jump to any conclusions that it's the same people, but there may be a connection. Please let us know if you can think of anything, anything at all that can help us.'

Jack pops in but the police push him back. He looks on from the front door.

'Goodness.' He gasps as he looks at everything strewn over the floor. He gives out a big sigh. 'Let me know if I can help with anything, Marlene,' he says, as he waves her goodbye, leaving the police to continue doing their job.

'Thank you, Jack,' is all she can utter.

'We have already spoken with the other store holders,' says Detective Blyth. 'No one heard anything. It must've happened during the night.'

'What now?' asks Marlene.

'We'll wait for the investigative report and then contact you. Would you like us to pack up all the paperwork once we're finished, Marlene?'

'Yes please.'

'And once we're done can you please go over it just in case you see anything out of the norm? Please?'

'Yes, of course, of course,' she replies.

'By the way, Marlene, the Victorian Police Homicide Squad are now also involved. You may get a call from them shortly. They will be looking at all our files. But I'll still be on the case. Don't you worry. We will all do the best we can.'

Marlene gets dropped off at home, with an empty, queasy feeling in her stomach, and her head full of more unanswered questions, anger and more sadness. All of a sudden, like a bolt of lightning, she realises that this incident is more complex than she first thought, and realises just how much she doesn't understand. Who are these people? Where have they come from? And Nick? What was he doing to deserve this? And why take Alex? She fears for Alex's safety even more now.

Her head spins. All she can do when she gets home is cry. There is now only desperation and for the first time in her life she feels totally out of control. She feels her world spiralling into disarray and destruction; destruction that can never be repaired.

******

Chapter 17

It isn't grey, raining or even cold, as one would expect on a funeral day. It's warm and sunny. Summer brightness penetrates the bedroom early, way too early to get up, but rise they do. Grandpa Bill arrives, and Aida is very pleased. Now she has both Grandma and Grandpa to play with.

Staggering to the kitchen, Marlene finds Edna preparing breakfast, sporting a big apron to protect her new black dress, and her greying, thin hair pinned tight in a bun behind her head. A solemn good morning is all they can say, and a light hug for her father, as they sit down to tea and toast. Shortly after, clutching her soft doll, Aida makes her way to the kitchen.

With Bill and Edna now in light conversation, clutching her cup, Marlene stares out the window. She's in her own world of thought, perhaps reminiscing on the events of that horrible night, or even of the life she and Nick had dreamed about, now smashed. She wishes this day to be over, but nonetheless, owes it to Nick. And what about Alex? Shouldn't he be here with them? Where is he? Why haven't they returned him? Why haven't the police found him yet? And just as these thoughts take hold, she bows her head and sobs uncontrollably.

Bill, tired from the long drive and in poor health, retreats to the lounge room. Following him, Aida sneaks up and climbs onto his knee and he gives her a quick smile, almost hidden under his hairy face, with his big beard resting on his chest. She dare not tell him he looks like Santa, not today when he has tears in his eyes. And this time he doesn't tickle her like she expects. He is sad, just like her mummy and her grandma, and this makes her sad, too.

And it's a good thing, perhaps, that Nick's parents aren't alive to witness this. How awful it would be if they were. His only sibling, his brother Brian who Nick hadn't heard from for so long, is the only living family that Nick has. And Marlene ponders on whether she should notify him. Would he want to know? It's all too heavy for her think about, and she dismisses it for now.

Marlene didn't want a fuss.

'A quiet family service,' she instructs the funeral celebrant. The big black car parked outside waiting to take them to the service is 'over-the-top,' she mutters.

'I can't understand this,' Marlene says to Edna, with arms folded. 'We could've driven ourselves, you know.'

'It's easier like this, Marlene. We won't have to worry about the driving. We don't even know how to get there. Isn't it better they drive us?'

But lack of sleep and worry is taking a toll on Marlene and she has developed a short temper. Edna understands this, and is patient with her, but her patience is also starting to wear thin. Edna takes a deep breath, looks over at Bill and shakes her head. He doesn't say a word and stares at the floor.

Edna shows Marlene a telegram from Nick's brother.

'This arrived yesterday, Marlene. I didn't want to give it to you then. You looked so tired last night.'

There was never any closeness between the two brothers and she did not hold any expectations that he would attend the funeral. They have not seen or heard from him in a long time, and it is surprising to receive a message from him.

'How on earth did he find our address?' questions Marlene.

'I let him know,' responds Bill. 'I had his phone number. It was the right thing to do, to let him know his only brother has passed away. And also that his nephew is missing. He may have already seen it on the evening news, or in the papers. He needs to know.'

Marlene is not pleased, even though she knows her father is right.

She reads his message, and then reads it again, trying to find some solace in it.

We are deeply sorry for your loss, Marlene, and will try to visit as soon as we can. Love, Brian and Sherly.

Is that all? No mention of his name? As soon as we can! And what's that supposed to mean?

Marlene didn't expect any more from Brian and Sherly. After all, Brian moved away long before Nick himself was old enough to move too. After that, there was very little contact between them.

She opens the lid on the kitchen bin, next to the fridge, and throws the telegram in. After a quick gulp of her now cold tea, she gets ready to leave for the service.

Edna fixes Marlene's cardigan over her shoulders, adjusts the fringe on her forehead, and helps her collect her bag, keys and stuffs a bunch of tissues in Marlene's bag and also her own. She turns to Aida to make sure that she too is nicely dressed, combed, and off they go.

Sandy, standing by the front gate with car keys in her hands, ready to follow them, waves as they pass, but Marlene has her head down and doesn't see her.

Friends from the city arrive for the service, and neighbours gather, too. Local store holders are also present, as well as Jack and Lisa. The small chapel is quickly filled.

The entire school of Mount Beauty Primary congregates outside. Mr and Mrs Angus take a seat at the back of the chapel, and Miss Potter and the other school staff assemble the students outside by the open doors. Miss Potter puts her hand on Ed's shoulder just as the funeral car pulls up.

Seeing Nick's name on the board next to the front doors is surreal. Marlene can barely stand, let alone look, but she does. A long blank stare at his name, as if he were someone else, not *her* Nick. Aida walks beside her grasping her hand, and Edna and Bill behind her, almost expecting to catch her should she fall.

They solemnly take their seats at the front, oblivious to the large crowd that has gathered in Nick's honour. Her head slightly bowed, in arm's length of Nick's coffin; so close she can smell the small wreath of fresh cottage flowers and gum leaves lying on top of the coffin. On a flimsy stand in front of the coffin is a framed photo of a smiling Nick, young faced, almost 'alive', as if talking. Marlene takes a few glances at the photo, and sniffles in pain. She can't remember choosing the coffin, or the photo. It is all a blur to her.

'That's Daddy,' says Aida, when she too sees the photo.

With her head still bowed, drying her tears, Marlene puts her arm around Aida's shoulders, as Edna grabs Aida's little hand and squeezes it in hers.

The funeral service is short, as Nick would have wanted. The eulogy read by the celebrant describes him as a young man with a full life ahead for him. 'A life cut short,' he says.

Growing up with his only brother Brian, they both struggled when they lost their parents in their young years. He continues to describe the love Nick had for his wife and children, eager to start their new lives in this beautiful town. Even though he had only lived here a short time, he had made many friends. 'He was respectful and respected,' continues the celebrant.

But the sermon is muffled to Marlene. A constant heavy head full of worry for Alex, she doesn't hear a word and can only wish it to be over.

Detective Blyth and other police officers stand at the back of the chapel, looking around and over their shoulders, searching for possible clues to help with their investigation, not just of Nick's murder but also Alex's kidnapping. Marlene is unaware of their presence. All she does is sob, still in disbelief that this is happening, that this is real, that this has happened to her and her family.

'May you rest in peace.'

These last words initiate sniffling from the gathering, and more crying from Marlene, and Aida nudges closer to her. A sole vocalist sings Here I Am Lord as they slowly glide down the aisle and gather in the foyer to receive condolences from all in attendance.

Sandy and Marg are first to arrive back at the house. They prepare a table laden with plates of sandwiches, cakes, finger food, and the kettle ready for the boil. Edna changes her outfit, and joins them to help.

Marlene puts on a brave face to greet neighbours and friends as they sadly enter the lounge room, with the men spilling outside to the back yard, whilst the police officers stand outside the front of the house, checking everyone going in. Making small talk in soft voices, the awkwardness soon impels the visitors to leave, understanding that Marlene prefers to be alone. Sandy stays behind to help clean up. Marlene's nervous disposition is evident, and she gently encourages Sandy to go home, too.

'Thank you very much for all your help, Sandy. Mum and I can manage with cleaning up. You have been so kind.

Max can stay and play with Aida, if that's alright with you,' Marlene says.

'Alright, Marlene. I'll pop in tomorrow to see how you are. Max, don't stay too long, you hear.'

Sandy wipes her hands on her apron, folds it neatly into her hands and leaves after giving both Marlene and Edna a kiss on the cheek. As the front door gently closes behind her, Marlene lets out a quiet sigh and throws herself onto the couch, next to Bill.

With Aida now comfortably sitting on the rug with Max, foraging through the toy box, Marlene is comforted that Aida has a friend to distract her from the terrible recent events.

And for the first time in this past week, with her arms folded as she gazes at Max and Aida playing, Edna catches the glimpse of a slight smile on her daughter's face.

******

Chapter 18

With Bill returning home, Edna stays behind to look after Aida while Marlene makes several trips to the police station, the doctor and the referred police psychologist over the following days and weeks.

'Please bring another photo of Alex with you when you come in,' says the young constable.

The harrowing task of going over photos continues to give her pain. She runs her hand gently over each photo and the tears start again.

'Which one, Mum? What do you think? Are these nice?'

'Yes, they are dear. He looks gorgeous here.'

And Edna, too, has tears in her eyes.

Interrogations are intense and persistent. The questions still the same, with little helpful answers and senseless open-ended scenarios. Marlene is losing hope that now, two weeks after that horrible night, they seem to be nowhere near finding Alex, or finding out who shot Nick, and the reason why. Their searches have not found the murder weapon or the car the men drove. Everyone that is interviewed has never seen or heard of anyone named Yuri or Viktor.

The constable shows Marlene images of faces, some rough, some clean, all strangers to her. Marlene strains as they turn to the next image, and then the next one, and the next. She can't properly remember what the men looked like, she tells the officer. Everything happened so quickly. The fear was immense and she is angry that she cannot recollect the details that the police are asking her to recall.

'I think they were taller than Nick. Yes. They were. Big men, not fat, just big. Huge shoulders.' She lifts her arms up to show them how big their shoulders were.

'Their hair short, really short, almost shaven. Big, dark eyebrows and scary eyes. When Viktor came up close to me, his eyes were really, really scary. But if you were to see them down the street, they would probably look normal, like normal people do. You know?' she says as she blows her nose in her scrunched-up hanky.

Police, emergency services and volunteers continue to scour the town, surrounding parklands, the woods and into the High Country. Helicopters, police officers on mountain bikes and professional trekkers all join the hunt. Nothing is found. The search is expanded to neighbouring towns into Tawonga and Bogong. Kiewa River is also searched by police divers. Perhaps hoping to find the murder weapon or the lifeless body of a little boy? That thought terrifies her.

'He's got to be somewhere. Are you sure you've checked everywhere? Someone must know where he is,' pleads Marlene. 'I didn't choose Aida over him. He was snatched out of my hand. I tried to hold him, but Viktor took him. He snatched him, he did. He snatched him,' she repeats, almost trying to convince the constable.

Detective Blyth stretches out his hand and grabs hers. 'We know, Marlene. We are now expanding our search to further neighbouring sites. Hang in there Marlene.' He tries to give her some comfort. 'We have also checked airport departures, hospitals, motels and performed door-to-door knocks far and wide.' He continues. 'Everyone in town has been interviewed Marlene.'

It makes the situation more real when Alex's details are registered in the National Missing Persons database. It almost affirms that he possibly may never be found, just like all the other faces on the registry, and this thought sears her heart. His little face in amongst many others who are missing, lost and, perhaps even worse, dead. Marlene cannot think of this consequence. She is hanging on to every inch of hope that he will be found and returned to her soon, alive and well.

'The only thing left to do now is to televise the story on national television. What do you think Marlene? Are you up to it?' asks Detective Blyth.

'Anything. Anything that will find Alex. Someone must know something. Why can't you find him?' she shouts in frustration, as she blows her nose.

With her permission, they ask to put up missing persons flyers in and around town.

Marlene arrives home exhausted. All she wants to do is lie on the couch and close her eyes. She and Edna fight, shout over each other, say things that are not helpful and both end up crying in the end.

'I don't know, Mum. I don't know. Why do you keep asking me? He never spoke of the stuff he did at work. Please stop asking me. I've told the police everything I know.'

'What about Nick's family? Why don't we know anything about his family? And his friends? Have they been interviewed?'

'Please, Mum. I'm sure they have. Not now. Please.'

'What did they say that night, those two men, Marlene? Surely, they must've said something. Why on earth would someone want to take a little boy? Little Alex. He can't just have been taken for no reason.'

Edna is just as frustrated as Marlene. She too is hurting, realising that Alex may never be found.

It gets harder to believe the police when they say, 'We are doing everything we can'.

How can they be, if they haven't found Alex? And these men? Why can't they find them? Where can they be hiding him?

'He must be somewhere. He's got to be somewhere!' Marlene shouts as she bangs her fist on the table, her body tense and face red in fury. She has no peace. Her mind is constantly pinned on the events of that night. Her heart is smashed and her own anxiety also makes Aida very anxious and very scared of her mum when she's in this state.

Edna puts her hands on Aida's shoulders to comfort her and Aida swings round to bury her head in Grandma's apron. The stress is extreme.

With the funeral of Nick now over, Marlene's focus is on Alex. She replays the events of that night over and over, trying hard to pinpoint anything she may have missed. What were they saying to Nick? What were they wearing? What type of car did they drive off in? But nothing comes to mind and this frustrates and angers her. And again, she returns to that night. What could she have done differently? Why didn't she hang onto Alex tighter? Why did she let go of him? Did she really choose Aida over Alex? Could she really have made that choice?

Edna hears Marlene's car drive off at any time during the day and often at night. Her daughter scours the streets, not just of Mount Beauty, but beyond, in hope of spotting someone or anything that will bring Alex back. She is gone for hours and sometimes gone for days. She is seen putting up pamphlets at bus shelters, lamp posts, park benches and anywhere she can secure a pamphlet. She returns home exhausted, dishevelled, staggers up the stairs and throws herself onto her bed without a word spoken.

The pain is unbearable. Neighbours visit to offer comfort but Marlene doesn't care to see them; she just wants Alex to be found. She doesn't want anyone to visit. Not even the psychologist.

'Enough is enough,' she says to Edna. 'The psychologist is not helping. I can't keep reliving that night.'

Aida is becoming more and more aware of the lack of attention that her mother is giving her. And even though Edna does most of the hugging and caring, Aida wants her mum to hug her. She wants to see her mum smile and laugh. She wants her to be her mum. She dreams of spending time in the garden with her, tending to the vegie patch, or just resting on the letterbox talking to Sandy, like they used to do. And she wants her to read her favourite book.

'Give her time, Aida. She will be okay in a little while. Once they find Alex, she will be a lot happier.'

Aida looks up at Marlene, hoping to catch her looking at her, but Marlene is out of it, totally absorbed in her grief. Aida realises that sometimes her mum doesn't sleep in her bed. She finds her on the couch, where she was the night before when Aida went to kiss her goodnight. It seems she hasn't moved. She also notices the ashtray on the coffee table, half full of wasted cigarette stubs. A habit that Nick had successfully got her to give up.

Edna has to force her to take a shower and dress, otherwise she'll stay in the same clothes or dressing gown for days.

'You mustn't neglect her, Marlene. She is hurting too and she needs you, especially now,' says Edna.

'Yes, Mum,' Marlene replies. 'But I can't give up on Alex. I don't know where he is and what they are doing to him. What if he is hurting? What if he is calling out for me? He probably thinks that I chose Aida over him. I didn't. I didn't choose. He's got to be found.'

Aida quietly pushes on Alex's bedroom door, and sees his room untouched. With her finger over her lips, Edna encourages her to go in quietly. And Aida does, but just for a little while. She plays with his toys and carefully puts them back where Alex left them. This is her way of feeling close to him. Marlene doesn't need to know that Aida has been in his room. She notices that Flops is not on his bed and is somewhat comforted that he is with Alex. At least they are together, she thinks.

******

Chapter 19

The summons from the bank manager and subsequent visit to the bank confirms the worst.

'Take a seat, Marlene,' says Geoff, the bank manager, as he closes the door behind her.

'I know this is not the time to worry you with this, Marlene. But there are a few issues and I'm not sure if you're fully aware of them. Nick has a personal loan that is secured against the house. This was taken out soon after your mortgage was approved which was to cover the shortfall on the initial set-up costs for his business. On top of that, he recently opened up a credit card, which I believe helped fund fitting out the office. Here are the latest statements, Marlene. I'm sorry if this is too much for you to handle right now. What can we do to help you whilst you decide what to do about your financials? Have you had a chance to think about Nick's business? There are a few options we can look at. Is there someone you can lean on for advice? What about Jack, the solicitor next door to Nick's office? Maybe he can guide you? Can we meet again in a fortnight? Is that okay, Marlene, or do you need more time?'

'No, it's alright, thank you, Geoff. Yes, I do need to work out what to do, don't I?' she says with a pensive look on her face. 'I will speak with Jack. Thank you again.'

With a limp handshake and half a smile, she heads outside, leans against the red brick wall to gain her balance and nervously lights up a new cigarette.

Marlene had no idea that they were in so much debt. She left all the financials up to Nick and trusted he did the right thing. She is certain that Nick believed the business would adequately pay out all these extra loans once it got going. There was never any mistrust between them. And now with no income coming in, their savings are dwindling away. This strain adds to her already anxious demeanour.

'I need a job,' she says to Edna when she arrives home. 'And I need one quick. But how can I find a job in my state? Who on earth will employ me? I'll lose the house if I don't find a job soon. I'll lose everything. Everything we've worked for.'

Edna quietly listens, as she always does.

'Don't worry. Something will come up. Everyone in town knows your predicament. I'm sure with word of mouth you'll find something. Would you consider relocating back to the city? There'll be more work opportunities there,' asks Edna. 'And you can stay with us.'

'No way, Mum. When Alex returns, we need to be here for him,' she says, still convinced that Alex will return soon.

Edna looks away in silence and continues folding the clean clothes. She knows her daughter is right. But will Alex return? As much as Edna would like to believe that he will, deep down she has almost lost all hope, but she dare not let her daughter know this.

It's a very difficult time for Marlene, as school breaks up for the summer holidays. She sees children on bikes, playing outside, making their way into the woods from the path across the road. She imagines Alex amongst them. She looks at them intensely, as if to be looking for him. Surely he's not with them? *Is he?* she asks herself. Of course, he isn't. But still, she hangs onto every bit of hope.

Aida spends time playing with Max either at his house or hers. Sometimes, when Max isn't so shy, they venture outside, with Sandy watching over them from the top step of her porch.

But Aida is always on the lookout for Ed. She spots him carrying his cricket gear as he heads to the cricket pitch with his friends. She wishes she could go, but Max isn't up to it.

Sandy volunteers to help Marlene get Aida ready for school.

'I might as well get Aida's things for school too, as I'm getting Max's stuff.'

'Thanks Sandy,' says Marlene. 'That is very helpful. Let me know how much I owe you,' says Marlene, with some relief that she doesn't have to worry about this task.

'I'll put the kettle on,' says Sandy, when Marlene visits to give her the money for the school supplies she has purchased for Aida.

As Sandy prepares the tea, Marlene waits in the lounge room. Aida and Max are enthralled in a new game. Marlene looks around the room and can see that all the photos of Max's dad are missing. Not one photo in sight.

'That's strange,' she mutters to herself. Why would they be missing? Has Sandy moved them somewhere else, perhaps?

'Sandy, where are all the beautiful photos of Max and his dad?' she asks her when she comes back in with tea and cake.

Marlene notices an awkwardness and nervousness as Sandy tries to answer her. It's almost as if Sandy is surprised that Marlene has noticed them missing.

'Oh, I've moved them to the other room,' is her quick response, but Marlene isn't convinced.

Why on earth would she move them?

'Perhaps something has happened with Max's dad,' is Edna's response when Marlene tells her mum. 'Maybe she's fed up that she hasn't heard from him and he hasn't visited.'

'Yes, perhaps so,' says Marlene, not sure of her reasoning.

Children's laughter and screams penetrate through the open front door and windows, as they run down the street to the path and into the woods to play in the clearing. This sends Marlene further into depression. She can't bear to hear children's voices, especially their laughter, and even their crying sends her mind spinning. Her constant thoughts are with Alex; she almost has to convince herself that he is not outside playing with them. She has to believe that he is safe and happy as she waits for him to come home. She can't wait for the summer break to be over so that the children are back at school. She blocks her ears when the noise is too loud, and goes upstairs into Aida's bedroom at the back of the house to escape. With windows and doors shut and curtains drawn, she is lulled into sleep at the foot of the bed.

******

Chapter 20

The call from the hospital is very upsetting. Grandpa Bill has fallen and has broken his hip.

'Go, Mum. You need to be with him,' says Marlene.

Even though Marlene is a little upset that her father is ill, she is equally upset that Edna is going back, but is somewhat relieved that she can have the house to herself and Aida.

On the other hand, Aida is very upset. Who will play with her now? Who will give her hugs? In her mind, she is losing another person, yet again. She will be left alone with Marlene and this saddens her.

Edna nurses Bill for as long as she can at home, but it is evident that she can't continue caring for him. She is frail herself and he now needs special care. So, after many phone calls to Marlene, and advice from the family doctor, the difficult decision is made to place Bill into care. A room at the local nursing home, in walking distance for Edna, is secured.

'Don't worry, Mum. He will be well looked after and you need your rest, too. I don't want you falling apart.'

With Nick's murder, Alex's kidnapping, and the constant phone calls from Edna with updates on Bill's condition, Christmas and New Year seem to come and go, just like any other normal day. No Christmas tree or presents this year. And no New Year celebrations either.

Sandy and Max visit on Christmas Eve to give Aida a pack of colouring books, pencils, and a new Barbie doll, but the festivities are very low key.

It is the same in Sandy's home. Max's father is nowhere to be seen. No mail, no phone calls and no visits.

'Would you like to spend Christmas day with us?' asks Sandy.

Max and Aida both look up at Marlene and their gazes drop when she responds.

'No, thank you, Sandy. Aida and I will have a quiet lunch at home. I'm expecting a phone call from my mother to see how my father is going. We shall stay put this year.'

Sandy gives them both a hug. 'I understand, Marlene. Perhaps Aida can come play with Max in the afternoon.'

'Yes, of course,' responds Marlene, as she puts her hands around Aida's shoulders

'Will you be coming up for Christmas?' asks Edna when she calls Marlene.

'Not this year, Mum,' replies Marlene. 'We won't be celebrating this year. How is Dad?'

'He's not too good, dear. But he's being well looked after.'

But Bill's condition worsens. The phone call from Edna explains that he developed excess liquid in the lungs.

'Acute pulmonary disease, the doctor said.'

He is rushed into hospital, and a few days later, passes away.

'I'll come up and help you with the funeral arrangements, Mum,' says Marlene.

And again, they are all thrust into a sad world of loss.

Bill's passing to Marlene is nowhere near as devastating as losing Nick and Alex, but sad just the same. Marlene is still living very much in a state of disbelief, and now, losing her father, everything overwhelms her.

After helping Edna with the funeral and helping her settle into a routine without Bill, Marlene decides it's time to go back home. Aida is sad to leave her grandma, especially now that she is on her own.

'Are you sure you are going to be okay on your own, Mum? You can come and stay with us,' says Marlene.

Aida looks up at her grandma, hoping she joins them.

'I will be alright, dear. I will visit just as soon as I can,' Edna replies as she says goodbye.

******

Chapter 21

Mount Beauty is swarming with holiday-makers. The town is busy with people eating, cycling or just gathering for picnics at the pondage. Some leave to make their way up to the High Country, but others choose to stay and absorb its beauty.

'We are very busy at the shop,' says Sandy. 'I guess it's good for business, but I'm so tired when I get home.'

Max has been staying with Marlene and Aida whilst Sandy works extra days and longer hours, and Aida is loving having his company. So does Marlene. She's happy her daughter has someone to play with. If Aida can convince him, they venture to the clearing and watch Ed, Fred and Mark play cricket. But after a short time, Max is keen to return back to the comfort of his home, or Aida's, until Sandy picks him up.

******

Further visits from Detective Blyth bring no new updates. They are still trying to piece together all the bits of information they have collected, with no success. Nick's murder, Alex's kidnapping and the office break-in still remain a mystery. He brings in more boxes of paperwork collected from Nick's office and Marlene is given the task of going over them in detail.

'I will sort through these tomorrow. Thank you, Detective Blyth. I'll let you know if I find anything.'

'Can you remember anything, anything else that the two men said that night? Anything, no matter how insignificant, might make a difference.'

'No. Nothing at all, detective. I will let you know if I do.'

And with that, tilting his hat and throwing a wink and a smile at Aida, Detective Blyth leaves.

******

Chapter 22

Jack gets in touch with Marlene, and offers her a job. His business is growing and he needs someone to help in reception, he makes her believe. Even though it's not a role that Marlene has experience or interest in, she accepts. Initially a part-time role, he tells her it may develop into a full-time role, if the business grows, as he is expecting.

With help from her doctor and the police psychologist that she has now fully embraced, Marlene feels a little better. Sleeping tablets, therapy and antidepressants are certainly helping.

'I almost feel normal.' Aida hears her mum tell Sandy. 'I'm getting more sleep, which is good,' she says with a half-smile. 'I really need it. How else am I going to get through the day?'

Marlene asks Sandy if she can look after Aida whilst she's at work, but sadly Sandy declines as she herself has her own job to go to.

'It's okay, Sandy. I'll ask Marg if she can look after her.'

And thankfully Marg accepts.

'It's only Wednesdays and Fridays, Marg. And in a couple of weeks, she'll be at school.'

'That's quite alright, Marlene. She'll keep us company, and she is so sweet and well behaved. We'll love to have her.'

******

Chapter 23

And so their lives begin to take a different turn. The life Marlene had planned and dreamed of with Nick has disintegrated.

The crying and night screams that Aida hears from her mum's room are a constant reminder of the sad events of that night, and time hasn't numbed the pain. Aida starts to accept that these may never go away. How can they? Their lives are changed forever.

The distraction of work is God sent in many ways for Marlene. With her salary now coming in along with money that Edna is sending, she is able to comfortably continue the repayments on the mortgage and pay for bills and food. Marlene is good at balancing her money, having picked up good budgeting habits from Nick. She struggles to make ends meet sometimes, but she knows that as she gets better she'll hopefully be able to increase her work days and bring in more money to help with all the financial commitments.

With Jack's legal advice, and help from the landlord, with mixed feelings, she terminates the lease on Nick's business. It meant so much to him, but she acknowledges this needs to be done. However, the matter of the personal loan is still outstanding, and is heavy on her mind.

'Oh, how Nick would be so disappointed to close shop,' she says to Jack.

'Nick wouldn't want you to carry this burden. I spoke with Geoff this morning and he has agreed to stretch the term of the remaining debt on the personal loan. This will reduce the payments and give you more time to repay it. All you have to do is go and see Geoff and sign the paperwork. In the meantime, I will place an ad in the local newspaper for the office equipment, and the funds can be put towards the loan. Is that okay with you, Marlene?'

'Thank you, Jack. Yes. You have been so helpful.' She gives him a long hug.

She is so grateful for this assistance. The whole community is behind her and in no time all the office equipment is sold and the office is cleared. Wayne and Jack volunteer to clean the office up before handing the keys back to the landlord. Another closure on her past life.

'We'll manage,' she whispers to herself on the way home to pick up Aida. 'We'll be fine, Nick.'

She doesn't at all think it's strange that she constantly talks to Nick, as if he is walking beside her.

The days seem to pass and roll into each other. Almost in robotic form, Marlene has her new routine down pat. Early morning rise. Wednesday and Fridays Aida runs up the road to Marg's, whilst Marlene lags behind her.

'Bye, Mum.' Aida waves as she reaches the gate to Marg's.

'Bye, Aida. You be a good girl. See you later today.'

Aida is not just happy to be with Marg; she is happy she gets to spend time with Ed. She loves to sit at the breakfast table, watching him scoff down his cornflakes, before grabbing his wickets and ball, giving his mum a quick kiss, and rushing out the door to meet up with Fred and Mark to play cricket. Aida follows him to the front gate.

'Bye, Ed.'

Ed doesn't respond. He just nods and keeps running.

After Wayne heads off to work, Aida and Marg stroll into town to pick up fresh supplies and pop in to say a quick hello to Marlene if they can see that she doesn't look busy. If she does look busy, Aida goes up close to the shopfront window, squishes her nose against it and waves to her. Aida loves doing this.

When they get home, she watches the children's programs on the television, before helping Marg set the table for lunch. She waits by the front gate, staring down the path for Ed to come.

She jumps in excitement as she sees him appear.

'Here he comes, Marg. He's here!' she yells. 'Can I go with him after lunch, Marg? Please?'

'I'm sure that will be okay, Aida. As long as you stay out of the boys' way.' Marg smiles, not knowing whether Ed will be happy with this arrangement.

Ed's feet briskly pick up pace, eager to get home, have lunch and get back to playing. After he has eaten all his sandwiches and gulped down his milk, he runs out, slamming the flywire screen behind him. Aida watches his every move and, quick as a flash, runs after him.

'Aida, go home,' he shouts.

And without paying any attention to him, she keeps running, finding her favourite spot on the big rock by the side of the clearing. With feet dangling, and a slight hum, she watches them.

'It's her way of being close to Alex,' says Marg to Marlene when she arrives to pick her up. 'No doubt she misses him.'

'Well, I'm hoping that she'll make new friends when she starts school,' responds Marlene.

Life develops into a continuous, mundane routine. Work for Marlene is soon increased to include Monday. She is grateful for the extra money.

Detective Blyth pops in every now and again to give her updates but even though he tells her they are still 'onto it', she has almost lost all hope. There has been no interest or leads. Alex and his captors seem to have vanished — vanished into thin air. Television and media releases have not unearthed anything new, something that Marlene and the investigating team find frustrating. Unfortunately, Marlene knows that police effort will dwindle as time passes. They will give up. This is her fear.

At night, when Aida is asleep, Marlene sneaks into town to put up extra fliers. She tapes these over the old tattered ones, now torn and faded with the weather. She doesn't want Alex to be forgotten.

With so many tourists around town now, she hopes that someone will recognise him. She clings onto every inch of hope.

******

Chapter 24

The beginning of February sees Aida start school. She can barely contain her excitement as she gets dressed in a new, blue chequered summer dress. She has breakfast standing at the end of the kitchen table, inching herself closer to the front door, as she puts her school bag over her shoulders.

'Yes, Mum. I have everything,' she says, as she heads to the front gate.

Marlene and Sandy walk Aida and Max to school. They see Ed riding up ahead of them and Aida wants to run up to him, but Marlene holds her back.

'Hey, you, let Ed go. You and Max can walk together to school, seeing that you are both in the same class.'

'She's very attached to Ed,' says Sandy.

'Yes. Too much. I guess he's her substitute big brother. Ed is a good boy, but she needs to make new friends and leave him alone. Hopefully school will do this for her.'

'Good morning, Miss Gladstone,' says Marlene as she accompanies Aida into the classroom.

'Morning, Mrs Bennet. Morning, Mrs Taylor. Come on, Max. You can sit here next to Aida,' says Miss Gladstone, as she takes Max's hand.

The teacher has already been informed about Max's anxiety in starting school and she tries to make him feel comfortable and safe.

'He'll be alright, Mrs Taylor. No need to worry. Just needs a bit of time,' she says to Sandy.

But Sandy has a very worried look on her face. She knows he will struggle. She doesn't want Max to notice her worry and smiles at him as he sits next to Aida.

Once all the children are settled and nestled together on the floor and engrossed in Miss Gladstone's storybook, Sandy and Marlene make their way into town for work.

'He'll be alright, Sandy,' Marlene reassures her.

Aida quickly makes friends and is very happy that she and Max are in the same class and so is Max. She feels like a big girl comforting and having him close, but sometimes Miss Gladstone hovers over her and Aida doesn't like this. She wants to be treated like the other children, not like a 'special' child that needs constant reassurance.

'She keeps asking me if I'm okay,' she says to her mum.

'She's just making sure that you are, that's all. I'm sure she also asks the other children. It is all new to them too, you know, Aida.'

But Marlene knows exactly why Miss Gladstone is asking. The terrible events of that night sent shockwaves throughout the town, and are still fresh in everyone's mind. Miss Gladstone is very aware of the effect that this may have had on Aida.

For the first few days, Max clings to Aida. But as the days progress, Aida starts to play with the other girls, and Max tags along, but her eyes are constantly on the lookout for Ed. She spots him, as he does her, but he is captivated by his cricket game and certainly doesn't want to be distracted by Aida. Deep down he does care for her, harbouring a sense of protection, staying close to her as his link to Alex, never giving up hope that one day he will be found.

Sandy is grateful that Aida keeps Max close by, even if he is spending a lot of time with the girls.

'He's doing alright Sandy,' assures Miss Gladstone. 'He's getting there.'

And he does. He eventually befriends classmates he can play ball and chasey with, and sometimes Aida joins him on the play equipment, but she'd rather be playing with her new girl friends. When she misses Alex, she hangs out near the cricket pitch to watch Ed. Oh, how she wishes that Alex was here, too.

Sandy likes to pick Max up from school every day. When Marlene can't be at school pickup, Aida goes home with

Sandy and Max, until Marlene finishes work.

'Thanks, Sandy,' yells Marlene when she gets home. She appreciates and recognises that without help she would struggle to keep a job and look after Aida on her own.

And Aida and Max treasure their time together, sprawled on the carpet munching on biscuits whilst watching afternoon cartoons as they wait for Marlene.

'Bye, Max,' yells Aida, hurriedly picking up her school bag as she hears her mum's voice.

There's no reply from Max; he's transfixed on the cartoons.

******

Chapter 25

It's time for me to move, Marlene. This house is too big for me now, living on my own. I want to move into a unit. It will be easier for me to maintain. What do you think, dear?' says Edna over the phone.

'I agree, Mum. You don't need a big house, and you certainly can't look after the garden now.'

So, with Marlene's support, Edna sells her home of forty-five years and moves to the outskirts of Melbourne, into a two-bedroom unit. Marlene and Aida drive up to help her pack and move. A lot of the furniture is sold or given to the Salvation Army, and a few boxes of mementos and special heirlooms are boxed and put into the boot of Marlene's car. Marlene is not sure what she's going to do with these, but she makes Edna happy by taking them off her hands.

'It's so good to get rid of all these things,' says Edna. 'I could never fit them into my little unit.'

Edna feels relieved that Marlene has come to help. Not just for herself, but as a distraction for Marlene and Aida, even if it is only for the weekend.

'I love your new home, Grandma,' says Aida, inspecting every room and the little garden patch outside the kitchen.

'Yes, Aida. This is just perfect for me. And when you come and visit there is a room for you and Mummy. I will make sure it is comfortable for you both.'

Aida smiles, because she knows that Grandma *will* make it special for them.

Yet that was not the only reason for Edna's move. She can see her daughter's struggle in trying to make ends meet, and some of the money she has left over from the sale of her house, after purchasing her unit, is given to Marlene.

'It will help you with your mortgage, Marlene. After all, what am I going to do with it? It's what your father would want, too.'

'Oh, Mum. Are you sure? You may need it yourself one day.'

'I have a bit saved for emergencies,' she replies. 'Don't you worry about me. It was inevitable that I had to move out of the big house eventually.'

The goodbyes are sad. They all don't know when they'll see each other again. With Aida at school, and Marlene now working five days a week, free time is limited. Edna is at an age where the long drive to Mount Beauty is difficult, and so the goodbyes are very emotional.

'We'll come and visit when Aida is on school holidays, Mum' says Marlene. 'I'm sure Jack will give me time off.'

'That's okay, dear. I'll be here.'

Edna stares as her only daughter swings into the front seat of the car. She notices how thin and gaunt she has become. Her hair long and unkept. Her skin and nails dry. She worries about her state of health and the strain she is under and hopes the financial assistance she has provided will help her. And Aida? Who is looking out for Aida? All this is so worrying for Edna. But, reluctantly, she waves goodbye, with throw-away kisses to them both as they drive off.

'Bye, Grandma. Love you,' she hears as they turn the corner.

The drive back home to Mount Beauty is melancholy, but happy. It seems to Marlene that Edna is settling into her new home well, and Marlene and Aida are in good stead to live more comfortably now that a portion of the mortgage can be paid off. With Aida falling asleep just as the sun goes down, Marlene contemplates her future.

******

Chapter 26

Most of the weekends are spent meandering through the wooded area into the clearing, where Marlene and Aida have a picnic lunch, or just lay on the grass absorbing the sunlight and mid-autumn breezes before the onset of winter. When the boys are playing cricket, Marlene and Aida watch in support. Marlene's mind is constantly on Alex, wishing he too were playing cricket with his now perfected spins, just like Nick taught him.

As the sun starts to hide, they brush themselves off and wander toward home, in and out of the bushes, in silence, on the lookout for anything suspicious, or maybe hoping to see a lost little boy making his way home; a wish for Marlene that is perhaps too farfetched, but worth dreaming about nonetheless.

Marlene tends to the garden sporadically, only when she really feels like it, or when the weeds are too tall and in the way of the pathway to the front porch. She plants the Japanese maple before winter sets in, just as its last leaves fall off their branches. She trims the roses lightly and piles all the garden rubbish in a corner of the garden, hopeful that one day she will cart this to the tip.

The days blend into each other with the same routine. First-term parent and teacher interviews show that Aida is progressing well through school and with this assurance Marlene can spend her time focussed on Alex; he is never far from her mind.

She often goes to the public library to scan through news events, not just in Australia but worldwide, just in case a little boy has been found. She spends hours scouring over microfiche files, asking library staff where the latest worldwide news clips are kept; doing a little of her own investigative work, just to make her feel less anxious and worthy.

As time passes, Aida can see that Marlene is always in a sad, pensive mood and she tries to cheer her up.

'My best friend is Julie, Mum. We play together all the time. When the boys play cricket, we run up to the fence and cheer them on. Julie's brother Fred is Ed's friend. You know? The little boy that always comes to Ed's house. They don't like us girls hanging around and watching them play cricket, and when they see us, we run away,' she says, giggling.

'You need to leave the big boys alone, Aida, especially if they are playing their game. They don't want distractions.'

Aida soon discovers that just as much as some friends can be kind, others can be hurtful. She gets teased about what happened to her father and her brother. This sends Aida crying to her teacher and sometimes the hurt is so bad she ends up in the sick bay, throwing up, her little body shaking.

Marlene is called to come and pick her up. *There is no escaping from this*, Marlene anguishes.

A new start in a new location would probably be better for both of them, but even if they were to move elsewhere, how would Alex find them? Moving house is not an option, Marlene believes. They cannot move. They need to stay here in case Alex comes back. It is something that Aida will have to learn to live with.

'Her teachers are all too caring, but ultimately, she will have to learn how to handle these nasty comments that some children throw at her,' says Marlene to Sandy.

'Hopefully, yes,' responds Sandy. 'There is really not much more to say. How can you stop children from being children?'

'Don't forget Father's Day stall is on this Sunday, children,' Miss Gladstone says, as she distributes notices of the stalls and activities.

The children are excited as to what they can buy their father, but Aida and Max are not. They retreat to their seats. Max looks down at the floor whilst Aida puts on a brave face. And in an instant, like a flash in her mind, she can hear the loud BANG that pierced the night, the loud BANG that pierced her father.

Father's Day, her father's birthday and Alex's birthday are not happy reminders. And to some extent she is comforted that she has Max near her who is experiencing the same feelings, and together they get through it.

'Okay, children. Turn to page twelve of your English book,' says Miss Gladstone, as a distraction for the other children, well aware of Max's and Aida's feelings.

Sunday soon arrives as the locals casually wander up to the school grounds for the yearly Father's Day BBQ. But not Max and Aida. Sandy briskly walks to work, as Max and Aida rush to the clearing. Marlene slumps herself into the hammock and escapes into her own little world.

But as the years move on, Aida's friends drift away and new friends come into her life. A constant change of friendships, not enabling her to have a true, long-lasting friend as such — something she yearns to have.

She misses Ed when he finishes primary school to go to high school. She misses riding to school with him and it's just not the same with only Max beside her. She can sense Ed's void in the playground, and the boys that play cricket now don't interest her as much as if it were Ed playing.

Most play times she joins in to play with the other children, but occasionally she prefers to sit by herself and watch everyone else play, laugh, scream or dance around her. Her quiet time is her special space where she can just switch off and not think of anything or anyone. Perhaps it's her way of protecting herself from hurt, from what the other children may think of her, the whispers sometimes too loud to ignore. Feet dangling, swaying gently on the swing, swishing sand around in the sand pit, or just sitting on the bench, munching slowly on an apple is her time.

And as she grows, she grapples to understand her father's murder, Alex's disappearance and why this has happened to her family. She wants so much to be like the other children, having a father and siblings. She misses calling out to her 'daddy', and Father's Day is empty and purposeless, as are all celebratory dates, including her birthday, forever etched in dread.

She wonders what her life would be like with her dad and Alex still around. She goes through emotions of anger, rage, sadness and self-pity. The silent tears she cries in her bed bring her no comfort, as does the empty room next to hers. She finds it hard to sit on Alex's bed now. The sadness is too much to bear, and her visits to his room become less frequent.

With her mother's health deteriorating, Aida also experiences spurts of depression. Feeling that she doesn't quite fit in, not just at school, but at home too. Her school grades are 'constant — not great, but just enough to see her through,' says the teacher at the last parent/teacher interview when she completes year six.

Marlene is not too worried; as long as she is managing and staying afloat that is all she can expect from her.

Aida is also not worried. She hopes that moving onto high school will be a new start, with new friends to bond with, and, to some extent, is looking forward to it. And she'll be back with Ed, riding to school together.

******

Chapter 27

Aida and Max both join Bright High School and, once again, are thankful that they are placed in the same class. She befriends Beatrice and Penelope who become her best friends, but this friendship doesn't last long. Different personality types, 'drama queens' as Aida describes them to her mum. Their interest in boys is much more than Aida's interest. So Aida doesn't really have a true friend for life, like she wants. And it is still Max and Ed that she turns to. There's a loneliness about her that seems to linger. The strong void evident, with the loss of her father and the kidnapping of Alex all those years ago, hovering like a dark storm following her, waiting to explode.

'Ed and Max are my best friends,' she says to her mother. 'Beatrice and Penelope have boyfriends. They don't want to hang around me anymore, Mum,' she says lowering her head with a sad face.

'That's okay, Aida. Friends come and go. You'll make new friends,' says Marlene, as she lights up yet another Marlboro and retreats to the porch.

Marlene silently swings into the hammock on the porch and shuts out the world.

Aida can tell that her mum's mind is not on her dilemma. Marlene's once again lulled into her world of sadness and pain.

Aida observes her, watching from the lounge window, and contemplates what she may be thinking or feeling, consuming one cigarette after another. The autumn wind carelessly blows her hair across her face. One leg dangling over the hammock, watching the clouds go by. The years have not been kind to her mother. The dreadful events of that night, even though many years have passed, have zapped her energy and excitement for life. Aida doesn't know whether to worry about her or whether to pity her. What can she do?

'Oh, Mum,' Aida whispers to herself, as she continues to stare at her through the window. 'I wish I could help you. I wish I knew how to.'

Aida could think that she too has lost her zest for life, but she hasn't. Perhaps the hope that Alex will one day return keeps her going. The distraction of school and catch-ups with Ed and Max keeps her mind occupied. And when she's really down she's called to the clearing by the boy's shouts and screams as they enthral themselves in their cricket game. That's not to say that Alex is not on her mind, especially when she imagines him playing with them.

'Night, Aidie,' she whispers to herself, almost believing that it's Alex saying this from his room when she can't get to sleep at night.

She wonders if he is also awake, like her, finding it hard to fall asleep or whether he is playing cricket somewhere far away. She wonders if he is planning his way home, where he belongs. She dare not think of any other consequences that may have become of him. The smiley face of a little six-year-old, so full of energy, clear in her mind.

'Tickle me, Daddy, tickle me.'

She remembers all too well her happy childhood years with her mum, dad and brother, and with these thoughts, cries herself to sleep.

As she gets older, she has flashbacks to that night and can see Alex tightly held by Viktor yelling, 'Choose, Choose,' and can hear her mum say, 'No, please, no,' and then hears the loud bang. And as these fearful thoughts enter her mind, she puts her hands over her ears, squeezes her eyes tight and silently hums, till her mind goes elsewhere. She has almost perfected this escape and most times it works, releasing her from the pain she feels.

When Ed has free time, she hears him call out to her and they jump on their bikes, head to the clearing and lie on the harsh, dry grass, and talk about where Alex may be and what he may be doing. They never talk of him as not being alive, and always with hope that they will be reunited.

'He will beat you, Ed, you know that,' she says. 'He'll bowl you out.'

Ed chuckles. 'I wonder how his injuries are. They would have healed by now, do you think?'

'Oh, I'm sure they would have,' responds Aida in a convincing tone.

And when they've had enough of a rest, they jump back on their bikes and speed down the dirt track, alongside the Western Highway, and belt down the slopes, around the corners, and when exhausted, turn back and make their way slowly back home.

These special moments are precious and healing to them both and it's evident that they both miss Alex so much. Aida treasures this time. It's an opportunity to be able to talk about Alex without her mum getting upset, sharing her feelings that are so similar to Ed's.

But as Ed progresses further into his high school years, he pursues his studies and cricket, and opportunities to spend time together like they used to become scarce.

Aida can understand this and deep down she knows that he will always be there, if she needs him. Her substitute big brother.

******

Marlene hasn't told Aida that she has stopped seeing the psychologist, nor has she told her that she has stopped taking the antidepressants. *A fourteen-year-old doesn't need to know,* Marlene thinks.

But Aida has noticed that her mum has changed back to the dreaded old days.

'Make my mind fuzzy,' Marlene says to Sandy, when they have a chat over the fence.

'But, Marlene, you may need them just for a little while longer.'

'I'll be right, Sandy. Honest. I've taken them for so long, I think it's time I let them go. No need to worry about me, Sandy. I'm fine.'

******

Chapter 28

Aida relishes the attention her grandma gives her when they visit during the summer break. Marlene is distant, always in her own world, and that has created a void that makes Aida ache. Aida can truly treasure the time she spends with her grandma.

Marlene is initially reluctant to go. At the back of her mind she's always thinking she needs to be home in case Alex returns, but Edna is insistent on them spending time with her. Not so much for Edna, but for Aida, who has missed out on so much.

'Just come up for Christmas Day, Marlene. You can leave the next day. I just want to spend Christmas with you both,' says Edna.

Aida's Christmas wish is always the same, and she is sure her mum's wish is the same as hers. But, unfortunately, it's a wish that Santa has never fulfilled. *Why would he now?* she questions.

Presents offer short immediate surprises, but no comfort. At night, when she settles into bed, she never forgets to wish Alexi a good night, like she has been doing since his kidnapping, every night and every year since.

It becomes quite clear to Aida, after her fifth, sixth and seventh birthday and in the years that follow, that she can never celebrate her special day like others do. Falling on the same day her father was killed and Alex was kidnapped — events that Marlene wants to erase from her mind forever — means no celebrations on her birthday.

'You can have a few friends the following week, Aida, but not on that day. Do you hear me?' is Marlene's determined reply every time Aida asks to have a birthday party on her actual birthday.

Marlene stands firm on this decision. As a child, Aida could never understand why, but now as an adolescent, it is clear to her that Marlene does not want them to have fun on such a tragic day.

Sometimes, Max quietly whispers, 'Happy birthday,' but this has to be in secret, so that Marlene does not hear. He always remembers her birthday and so do Sandy and Ed.

Sandy is often tempted to bring home a cake for her, but she doesn't, for the respect and friendship she has with Marlene.

Aida, Max and Ed ride their bikes to the clearing, lay on the ground and both Max and Ed sing her happy birthday, adding in their laughter after each line.

Oh, how appreciative she is of this. But her mind always goes to her father and then to Alex.

And Alex's birthday. How is this celebrated? Marlene wanders off to Kiewa River on Nick's and Alex's birthdays. She never asks Aida to join her.

Aida imagines her crying and whispering, 'I didn't choose, Alex. I didn't choose.' This torment, eating away at her, every single day.

Ed is never too far away, becoming a part of her family just like Sandy and Max are. He comes to the house to drop off his mum's cooked meals. He doesn't mind. His wish is that one day it will be Alex answering the door.

Aida finds excuses to be with him by asking him to help her with homework. Now that she is in high school, she finds school-work difficult. Homework in particular is challenging, requiring concentration and motivation, something she lacks and struggles with. Ed seems to have a knack of explaining things for her to understand and grasp.

Perhaps her need for his help spurs him to continue to visit; a comfort she craves, almost a substitute for Alex's presence.

It is a comfort for Ed, too, that he is helping Alex's little sister, watching over her, like Alex would want of him. They lie on the floor with school books spread open and notepads scribbled on, and when they are both tired of doing homework, they dash to Ed's house and play Pac-Man.

Marlene doesn't notice them leaving. She aimlessly cleans up in the kitchen, dazed out, with a cigarette hanging out of her mouth, something that Aida is quite embarrassed about.

Aida's Saturdays are filled with anticipation when watching Ed play in the Mount Beauty cricket matches, usually against other surrounding community teams; Bright, Myrtleford and even as far out as Wangaratta. She travels to the matches with Marg and Wayne, chatting nervously all the way up and back.

'She's no trouble, Marlene,' says Marg when they return home late.

But winter is dreary. With Ed heavy into his studies, Aida turns to Max, often paired with her for school assignments. Completing homework in her bedroom, or she in his, not just working on school assignments but slowly developing affectionate feelings for each other.

He never talks about his feelings and has a vulnerability and weakness that she can't explain. He knows all of Aida's pains and challenges, but she doesn't know much about his. She questions whether this is why she is drawn to him. He never talks about his father and Aida never talks about hers to him. Isn't it strange, she thinks, that neither of them can talk about their fathers? As if it's a taboo subject; an understanding they have not to 'go there'. Is it protection from pain? These past eleven years, she has never seen Max's father visit. She wonders how this affects him and deep down feels sorry for him, just as sorry as she feels for herself not having her father and brother.

Ed on the other hand is strong, not just physically, but mentally as well. He excels at school and graduates with honours, allowing him to enrol into university.

Aida is not surprised he has done so well, but is sad that he will not be living close by after he finishes his last year of high school. She is sad that she will not be able to watch him play cricket, representing the Mount Beauty Cricket Club, something that no doubt Alex would also have been a part of. She is proud and happy of Ed's success.

'Look, Aida. We've made the local paper. We beat Myrtleford again. Three years in a row. How good is that?' he says enthusiastically, as he flicks through the sports pages.

Aida laughs and looks straight into his eyes, gleaming with happiness.

'And, next year, I'm hoping to join the Victorian Cricket Club. That's if they select me.'

'I'm sure they will, Ed. You are so good at your game, and so passionate,' she says, as she puts her arm around his back.

Ed takes a deep sigh and then, with a huge smile on his face, gives the top of her head a rough rub.

'He wants to study law,' says Marg to Marlene. 'He is very lucky to be accepted at La Trobe in Albury. It's not too far for us to travel and visit him.'

Marg's pride is evident in the tone of her voice, and Marlene also feels very proud of him.

Marlene and Aida walk up to Ed's house on the day of his move to Albury. They watch as Marg and Wayne help him load his newly bought car, purchased from Bob's Second Hand Cars in town. Busily securing his bike onto the bike rack, Aida stops and stares at him. He looks so grown up and mature. It seems like he has become a man all of sudden. No longer the little boy that played cricket with Alex. No longer the boy that helped her with her homework.

She is absorbed by his every move, organising things in the back seat of the car and squashing bags and a suitcase into the boot. She tries hard to hide the aching smile on her face, and can't help but get teary as he comes up to hug her goodbye.

'See you around, Aidie,' he says with a little chuckle. 'I'll visit when I can. Catch ya. And don't forget to keep in touch.'

'Yeah, catch ya, Ed,' is all she can say.

Alex is the only one who can call her Aidie, but coming from Ed, she's comforted rather than annoyed.

And with that, she turns around to go home, listening intently as Ed says goodbye to Marlene and then to his parents. She bursts into tears as she hears the car drive off, and runs through her front gate and up to her bedroom, peering out of the window. He's gone. Her arms around her body, she realises another loss in her life. The quietness of the street and the quietness of her room engulfs her and she takes a few deep breaths to compose herself before her mum comes home.

******

Chapter 29

'Do you want to ride up to Bright this weekend, Aida?' asks
Max. 'I hear there is a fair and there will also be a live band
in the park. How about it? We can pack the tent and stay
the weekend. What do you think?'

Max can see she's down. Maybe he can sense her
feelings for Ed.

'That'll be nice, Max. Yeah, why not! Get away from
here for the weekend. I'll get my bike and stuff ready and
tell Mum. Meet you in five.'

A couple of t-shirts and a spare pair of jeans are
thrown in her backpack. She pulls the camping sack
out from the storeroom, takes some money from the jar
on the top kitchen shelf, and hastily jumps on her bike.
She follows Max through town, onto Simmonds Creek
Road, riding along Dungey Track into Bright. With Max
turning round every now and again to make sure she is

following, they decide not to stop and continue the two-hour ride, eventually arriving at Riverside Holiday Park. Her calf muscles burn in pain, and they decide to rest a while before heading into town.

'Gosh, Max. I'm so unfit. Haven't ridden this far ever. But what a beautiful ride it is,' she says, as she rubs her calf muscles.

'Sure is,' he responds, as he takes off his shoes and socks and does the same.

They find Bright Centenary Park filled with holiday-makers, which is not surprising for this time of the year. The locals have set up fete stalls with knick-knacks and food to go. The bands play loud, and Max and Aida get lost in the trance and the dancing, falling over when they are too engrossed in their crazy moves. They sit on the grass, eating, drinking and smoking cheap joints that Max managed to acquire from the group of young hippies at the back of the podium. Singing and leaning on each other as night approaches, with the bands now packing up, they stagger to their camp spot, their first-time smoking weed obviously not agreeing with them. They giggle and stumble into their tent. They are out for the night.

Their thumping headaches and queasy feeling wakes them early the next morning. The festivities on the park continue for the rest of Sunday but they are in no mood to party like they did yesterday. They lie on the grass, sipping bottled water until they feel better, before contemplating the two-hour ride back home. They buy cheap coffee and donuts, and listen to the music, escaping to their own little private world. The thought of her returning home is not happy. Her home is no longer the warm, loving home of long ago. Now it's a house she no longer wants to be in.

Cautiously following behind Max as they ride home, Aida is certainly not looking forward to seeing her mum and wonders what state she'll be in. She is tired of constantly looking out for her, and is tired of her excuses as to why she always looks dishevelled and worn out. Aida has given up on asking where she's been when she's gone all night. It has become so hard to live in the same house with Marlene. Each doing their own thing, as if strangers cohabitating under the same roof.

******

Chapter 30

The late-night telephone call from the Royal Melbourne Hospital startles Marlene.

'You'll have to hurry,' says the nurse on the other end of the phone.

Waking Aida, she frantically packs an overnight bag, and they are out the door in a hurry. But even speeding all the way doesn't get them there in time. It's too late. They are told that Edna passed away shortly after the telephone call. Disheartened and somewhat shocked, they are regretful that they were unable to say goodbye to her. Again thrust into a world of grief, sadness and the task of organising yet another funeral must be faced.

They stay at Edna's unit until she is cremated, and, as per her instructions, have her ashes scattered off Mornington

Pier, as were Bill's. A few of her precious personal belongings are packed in the boot, before returning home, harbouring a further sense of emptiness.

As Marlene drives the long ride home, Aida reflects on her past, trying hard not to focus on their misfortunes, but unwittingly she does. Rubbing her hands over her grandma's felt coat that she is wearing, a nervousness overcomes her. With her head turned to the left, leaning on the cold window pane so that Marlene can't see her tears, she watches as the all too familiar gum tree on the corner of the highway comes into sight.

What does she have left now? Her father taken far too young, and Alex still missing, there is now added pain with both Bill and Edna gone. And what about Alex? What's happened to him? Has he been forgotten? Surely not! And Ed? So caught up in his studies and his cricket it seems he has little time for her. Who can she turn to now? Marlene is so vulnerable, far too weak to help her; she's just barely holding up herself, let alone having strength to help Aida. It's unbelievable that there will be no more phone calls from Grandma to bathe her in love. She will no longer hear her loving voice and no longer be able to push her head into her apron and absorb herself in Grandma's smell, like only a grandma can smell. Losing herself in her warmth, dispersing all her demons, just for a little while at least. As her pain builds up, she lets out a loud cry just as they pull up to the house.

Max and Sandy are waiting for them by the front door. Sandy follows Marlene into the house, with a cooked meal, fresh milk and bread, whilst Max helps Aida unload the car.

'You won't have to rush into town, Marlene. This will see you for a few days,' says Sandy, as she carefully lays everything on the kitchen table.

'Very kind of you, Sandy. Always thinking of us. Thank you,' replies Marlene.

Shortly after, Marg pops in with more cooked meals. With the usual condolences said, she closes the door behind her, leaving Marlene and Aida each in their own thoughts, carrying their own private grief. They walk up to their rooms and sink into their beds for much-needed sleep.

'Hello?' Aida quietly answers the phone on her bedside table.

'Hi, Aida. It's Ed. I'm so sorry to hear about Edna's passing. Are you alright? Is there anything I can do? I can come over if you like.'

'Oh, Ed.' She bursts into tears and can hardly talk. 'I didn't get to say goodbye to her, Ed. She died alone in hospital. We tried our best, but we got there too late. I didn't get to say goodbye.' And the tears continue.

'She knew how much you loved her. Don't beat yourself up over it. You have to hang on to all the happy times you had together. That's what she would want of you.'

He is right, of course. So happy that he rang, Aida somewhat feels safe, knowing he is just a phone call away and willing to come over if she needs him to. Oh, how she misses him.

But after the phone call, Aida's mind is too awake to fall asleep. She is soothed by the light rain dribbling down the window pane and reflects on the last time her grandma visited. She can feel her warm hand around hers, and can hear her soothing words. Words that only a grandma can relay to her much-loved, only granddaughter. She closes her eyes, inhales deep into her grandma's coat, still wrapped around her, and imagines lying next to her. With Ed's words circling around in her head, she finally falls asleep, curled up into a ball, sideways on the bed.

Jack helps to finalise Edna's will and takes care of probate. It's stress that Marlene does not have to deal with. Not surprisingly, the unit and all its contents are willed to Aida, apart from Bill's war medals that are gifted to Alex. Monetary funds in Edna's accounts are left to Marlene and a trust account is set up to Aida in safe keeping for Alex.

'She was hoping that Alex is coming back,' says Jack to Marlene and Aida.

'Yes. She always said that he'll be found one day. She never lost hope. None of us have,' Marlene reassures herself. 'Thank you, Jack, for looking after this for us. And the money she left me will surely help,' says Marlene with a big sigh and teary eyes. 'It almost completely pays off the mortgage.'

A gift Marlene is most thankful for.

******

Chapter 31

But the stress, emptiness and loneliness cause more strain and distance between Marlene and Aida. Without Ed to turn to, Aida falls to school mates for distraction, spending much of her weekends in the school grounds, shooting hoops, or hanging out at the local coffee shop with the usual gang and then casually dragging herself home when it's time for the shop to close.

Tall and pretty, with fair features just like her mother, Aida attracts interest from the local boys and some throw advances at her at every opportunity they can get; advances that are uncomfortable to her. She is not interested in striking up a relationship with any of these boys, especially Mark, whom she considers a close friend of Ed's. She dismisses Mark's frequent requests for a date. She finds them annoying and unpleasant and, as these advances become persistent, she stops going to the hang-outs and turns to Max for comfort, spending more time at his house than her own. She spirals into a deep hole of despair. Ultimately leaving school, just months prior to completing her HSC, she plans her move to the city into Edna's unit. What she is hoping for or seeking is unclear to herself and Marlene.

'I don't know what I'll do, Mum. I will let you know once I settle in. I'll find a job first and continue my studies later. I just can't do it right now. I can't concentrate.'

Marlene understands all too well how her daughter is feeling. A mind full of worry, stress and anxiety doesn't leave much room to concentrate on other things in life. Marlene feels the emptiness that has taken over her and knows how hard it is to move on.

'Perhaps this is what you need, Aida. I'm sure it will do you some good,' says Marlene, comforting her with a soft squeeze of her arm.

Max is early the next morning. With his newly acquired driver's licence and a new car that Sandy has purchased him, he is ready to drive her into the city.

Aida looks around the house to see what else she may need or want to bring to the unit. She selects a few framed photos, books and knick-knacks that will make her feel at home. Without letting Marlene see, she also takes her mum's apron, hanging behind the kitchen door. Not that Marlene uses it a lot these days, but an item that will certainly make her feel as close to her mum as it can.

'You won't need much, Aida. The unit is still as Mum left it,' says Marlene.

And Aida is happy it is.

A peck on the cheek and a quick hug from Marlene and Aida's off. Marlene stares down the street, until the car turns into the highway.

Max stays overnight to help her settle in, but in the midst of end of school exams, he has to return home the next day.

'Are you sure you don't want to finish the year, Aida? It's our last year.'

'No, Max. I just can't now. I can repeat the year later if I change my mind.'

'I'll visit during the holidays, Aida. Ring if you need anything.'

They hug. Neither wants to let go. Max strokes her hair, as she gently rubs his back. With her head resting on his shoulders, she realises they are almost the same height and she smirks when she realises this.

'Gosh, Max. I'm just as tall as you are. I always thought you were taller than me.' She giggles.

'Well, you are pretty tall for a girl, you know.' He laughs back.

A kiss on her cheek and he's off. His hand out of the car window waving goodbye, till she can no longer see him.

******

Chapter 32

Marlene is left with too much free time on her hands now that Aida has moved out. She wanders around the dark house, looks into Aida's room, then closes the door. Heads to Alex's room and does the same. Both lifeless. Quiet. Empty.

She has lost her sense of routine. Can't quite motivate herself to do anything.

'Sorry, Jack. I'm not feeling well. Can't come into work today.'

Jack finds the all too familiar phone call disturbing.

She sleeps during the day, and the nights are spent lighting one cigarette after another as the empty bottles of Jack Daniels pile up in the kitchen bin. Her phone is often not answered, as is the front door when Sandy or Marg visit.

'I'll leave some fresh groceries by the door, Marlene. Ring me if you need anything,' shouts Sandy.

Marlene is so grateful to have Sandy looking out for her. She is in no state to see anyone, let alone venture out for shopping.

Sandy, though worried, understands this, and gives her the space she needs.

It's not just the death of Nick, her parents and Aida's move that pains her. It's Alex she is hurting for the most. Now that she is alone, she has more time to ponder on all these years gone by.

She wonders whether he is still alive, and this thought shatters her. Then she wonders what he would look like now. A grown man of twenty, almost approaching his twenty-first birthday; would she recognise him if he were to walk past her in the street? His little smiley face and effervescent laugh shrieking in her ear. And then her thoughts turn to Nick. A thriving business would now have been achieved. A proud man and loving husband and father, missing out on so much.

'Puff. Into thin air,' she says to herself. 'How can that be? How can he just disappear?'

She tortures herself with these thoughts of hopelessness.

The visits from Detective Blyth, now infrequent, are replaced by a phone call.

'We are doing our best, Marlene.'

'Yeah, sure you are,' she replies and then pauses. 'Tell me something, Blythy. What did he mean when he said,

"You didn't tell me there were two?" What did he mean by that? Tell me.'

'What are you talking about, Marlene? Who said that?' asks the detective.

'He said that! Viktor. He said it to Yuri. YOU DIDN'T TELL ME THERE WERE TWO,' she yells into the phone angrily.

'When did he say that? You didn't mention this before, Marlene. This is the first time I've heard this. When did he say that?'

'That night. He said it that night. What did he mean by that?'

'I'm coming over, Marlene. I'm on my way.'

He is accompanied by a young fresh-faced policeman, introduced as Constable John Brown, but Marlene pays no attention to him.

With a limp handshake and a cigarette hanging loosely on her lips, she tightens the robe around her body and gestures them into the lounge room.

'Tell me again, Marlene. What did you hear that night?'

'I think I heard *you didn't tell me there were two*,' she says, as Constable Brown scribbles in his little notepad.

'You never mentioned this.'

'I thought I had. Well, I thought I had. Why? What difference does it make?' she says, as she tilts her head up and blows out a thick puff of smoke.

'Well, it tells us that they didn't know there were two children in the house. It seems that they only expected one child to be here, not two.'

'That's why he said I had to choose. Does it matter?'

'It might. Is there anything else you can remember? Even small details may help.'

'No. I don't think so,' she replies.

'Did they call you by your names, Marlene? Do you remember if they knew Nick's name? Did he actually say his name?'

'Yes. He called him Nikolai. That's Nick, isn't it?'

'Nikolai is not Nick, Marlene. What about you? Did they say your name, or the children's name?'

'No. Only Nick. Only Nikolai. They didn't say my name or Alex's or Aida's. Only Nick's.'

Detective Blyth looks at Constable Brown, disturbed at what he's hearing, and makes sure he is writing all this down. The look on his face is strained and worried. After all these years, something new has come up. He's not judging, but finds it peculiar that Marlene is remembering this now.

But then again, he understands that trauma can do this. It can block certain events and Marlene has without doubt suffered extreme trauma.

'Have you gone through the boxes of paperwork? Did you find anything of interest? Was there anything missing?'

'The only thing I couldn't find in the boxes are our birth certificates. I'm pretty sure Nick said they would be safe in the office with all the other documents. I've looked everywhere in the house and have gone through the boxes in the storeroom. I remember that I took Alex's and Aida's birth certificates to the school office when I enrolled them. I had no need for them anymore, so Nick kept them in his office. But I can't find them. I assumed your officers took them.'

'No, Marlene. I'm pretty sure these documents were not found during our investigation, but I will double-check when I get back to the station. If you are sure they should be there, then they may have been taken. Perhaps that is what they were looking for at the office when it was ransacked. Are you sure nothing else is missing?'

'I'm pretty sure,' says Marlene.

'We will be in touch,' he says.

She shakes their hands and closes the door behind them.

She is too tired and confused to give this matter more thought. She has almost lost hope in finding Alex and believes this small piece of information is insignificant.

But Detective Blyth and Constable Brown do not think so. This is major and may help with Alex's search and solving Nick's murder.

With this new information, Detective Blyth applies for and is granted funds to re-instate a small team of detectives to have the case files re-checked. Airport, train and sea farer's records are double-checked. Why on earth would they need their birth certificates? And why did they call him Nikolai? Did they use these documents to produce fraudulent ones for themselves and Alex? With his enthusiasm reignited, Detective Blyth is determined to find answers to all these questions.

He rings the school to see if they have copies of Alex's and Aida's birth certificate and he is in luck.

'Yes, we do, Detective. We took copies of Alex's and Aida's birth certificates when Mrs Bennet enrolled the children.'

Excellent. A break-through, he thinks.

'I'll be right there,' he yells down the phone in excitement.

He wastes no time in going to the school office to collect copies. The main interest is to see what the registered names of their parents are on the certificates. He wants to see if Nick is registered as 'Nick' or 'Nikolai'. He also obtains a copy of Nick and Marlene's marriage certificate, and all other documents that display Nick's name: business name registration, home loan applications, everything.

'This will help,' he says with a huge sigh, as he slumps into the old armchair in Marlene's lounge room.

When they hear the kettle whistling, they retreat to the kitchen for a cup of tea before examining the documents Detective Blyth has in his folder.

He doesn't blame Marlene for not mentioning it sooner as he can fully understand the strain she suffered, and is still suffering. But, boy oh boy, this would've helped if she had mentioned it back then.

The weeks pass and Marlene doesn't hear from Detective Blyth and she dismisses all the excitement, continuing to live her days asleep on the couch and nights awake, pacing the dim-lit house, drinking and smoking. The neighbours notice the lack of movement in and around the house. The curtains are always drawn, and letters and junk mail overflowing in the letterbox. Her much-loved garden looks shabby and unattended.

Sandy clears out the letterbox when she visits, but the doorbell is mostly unanswered, so she slides the letters under the door.

'Oh, Sandy. Come in,' Marlene says, on the rare occasion that she opens the door to her.

Sandy is shocked at the state of the house. The sink is full with cups and glasses. There are cigarette butts squished in ashtrays all over the lounge room and kitchen. Empty whisky bottles in the overflowing bin, and Marlene has not showered in days, with her hair frazzled and dressing gown hanging loose over her thin body.

'Marlene. Let me help you. I don't have work today. We can spend the day together if you want.'

'No need, Sandy. I'm fine. Really.'

They sit and chat for a while, and Sandy notices Marlene's dark, baggy eyes, red and watery. Her once glowing skin is now blotched and her lips are cracked and dry, most likely from the constant cigarette smoking.

She talks nonsense and Sandy has to try hard to make out what she is saying. She observes her pulling on the robe belt, knotting it tighter and tighter, whilst balancing her cigarette on edge of her lips. Her hands twitch as she pushes her hair behind her ears, but it's so dry and knotted it quickly springs back onto her face.

Sandy feels sorry for her. She reaches out to grab her hands, but Marlene quickly stands up and moves toward the window, nudging at the curtain to take a quick peek. Sandy senses it's time to leave. She gives Marlene a gentle squeeze and heads off to see Marg.

'What can we do, Marg? She is in a terrible state.'

'There is nothing we can do unless she asks for help. Let's keep an eye on her. Have you rung Aida to let her know?'

'No. I don't want to worry her. I know she has recently started working and I don't want her to be rushing back and losing her job.'

******

Chapter 33

Aida has indeed started a new job. After weeks of rearranging the furniture in the unit to make it comfortable for her new life, her application as a receptionist for a young city-based psychologist is successful. It's just a short tram ride into town — it appears that this is the right move for her.

She thrives in the office environment, surrounded by young receptionists of similar age, working for other varying professionals scattered around the open floor space. She soon builds a new group of friends that she can socialise with after work and on weekends. It's soul-lifting and this new life, to some extent, is helping her escape the sadness and misery that has engulfed her these past fourteen years.

And even with this new start of life, she hasn't forgotten anyone at all. Her mind is always on Ed, wondering what he is up to, and on Alex, of course, wondering if he is still alive and well, or whether anything sinister happened to him that night, still so very clear in her mind. And when she arrives home after work, her surroundings immediately help her bond with Edna's spirit, always with her, she likes to think. She closes her eyes and digs deep to feel her grandma's touch, and she's content with these thoughts.

The phone calls back home to her mum become more and more infrequent. The distance between them increases, making it harder and harder to have a proper conversation. Marlene's constant focus is on Alex's disappearance, and she has almost forgotten that Aida is alive and still wanting so much to be loved and cared for.

Max visits as often as he can, and stays the night, sometimes more than one night. She loves introducing him to her friends, but his shyness is still a hindrance. He prefers to stay at home with Aida rather than go out for a night of fun with her work colleagues.

And sometimes, when they've both had too much to drink and feel lost in a sea of dread, they fall asleep together. With his arm strewn over her naked body after lovemaking, her mind rushes to Ed. How she wishes it was Ed beside her and not Max.

They both know this relationship is temporary. Leaning on each other for comfort as 'best friends' they soon realise their reality.

'It's not working, is it, Aida? I don't feel you have the same feelings for me as I do for you. Am I correct?'

'It's got nothing to do with you, Max. It's me. I'm stuffed. You are a great guy. I'm just not ready to commit to any relationship right now. There has been so much happening in my life, especially this last year settling here and starting work, I'm still finding my feet. I do care for you, Max, but perhaps not in the same way that you want me to. Can we still be friends? I really don't want to lose you.'

'You will never lose me, Aida.'

They huddle on the bed as he caresses her face, kissing her on the head and dreading the next day departure.

Her life resumes back to its normal pace after Max leaves. Happily working for Joan, mingling with her friends after work, and partying hard on Friday and Saturday nights, she discovers a world of entertainment, music and drinking. This new world revolves around work and fun times. She looks forward to the end of a working week, dressing up and partying; it gives her happiness that she hasn't experienced before.

She is prepared to try anything; anything that distracts her from her past life, embracing city nightclubs and new boyfriends that come her way. She meets many men and some join her back home for a nightcap, sometimes ending up in bed together. She doesn't call this lovemaking, as she definitely is not in love with them. It's pure sex. Distraction. A night of company, drinks and escape. She has no regrets with the decisions she makes. Encouraged by her new friends, she is living it up.

But deep down she harbours a feeling of guilt. Thinking of her mother, she questions if it is right that she should be having so much fun, whilst her mother is drowning in dread.

Emails between her and Max tell her that after finishing his HSC, he decides to travel. He takes the coastal road to New South Wales, where he does casual work for a while, and then travels up north to Queensland. Aida is happy for him. It's as if the shy little boy she shared school with is all grown up.

'Wow. I'm so happy for you Max,' she says when he rings her throughout his trip. 'You must send me photos. When do you think you'll be coming home?'

'Not for a while, Aida.' He chuckles. 'Maybe for our twenty-first. I want you to celebrate it with me.'

'Okay, Max. We will.'

And with that, she hangs up and for the first time ever she is happy that she can finally plan a birthday party.

And she understands why Ed doesn't keep in touch as often as she would like. This last year of his law degree is gruelling and she doesn't want to distract him by calling or emailing him too often.

'Guess what, Aida?' Ed asks when he rings her. 'I'm going to London. The Victorian Cricket Club want me to join them when they go up next year. I need to finish my degree though.'

'Oh, wow, Ed, that is fantastic! I always knew you were going to make the team.' She giggles.

'I'm going home for Christmas this year. If you're there, I can see you then.'

'I'll see how I go with work. I'd love to see you, Ed.'

His excitement is overwhelming. She can sense it in his voice. She flops onto the couch after their conversation ends, and realises just how much she misses him. She wonders if he misses her, too.

But when the night loneliness engulfs her, she thinks of her mother.

'Mum. You haven't called in a while. Are you okay?' she asks one night over the phone.

'Yes, Aida. I'm fine. No need to worry.'

'I've got a new job, Mum. I'm still working for Joan, but she has given me a new role and a pay rise. Isn't that great? And guess what? She's encouraged me to take up part-time studies; a counselling course. I don't know if I'm up to it, but I'm giving it my best shot. She's helping me with my subjects. What do you think, Mum?'

'I think that's wonderful, Aida,' she says half-heartedly.

'Well, night school is keeping me out of mischief. It doesn't leave much time to party.'

They talk about the weather, and catch-ups around town. Aida tells her how busy the city is, and how much she misses the quietness of country living, and Marlene agrees.

'Mum, is your computer connected? l can send you some photos of my new car.'

'Oh, you know I'm not good with computers. You can show me when you visit.'

'Okay, Mum. How is everyone back home? Have you seen Max? I haven't heard from him lately. I've sent emails, but he hasn't replied. Is everyone okay?'

'Max is in Queensland. Sandy said he has better work opportunities, so he might be settling there. He's coming down later in the year, but this time he'll be coming with his new girlfriend to introduce her to Sandy. Did you know he has a girlfriend? They are planning to marry, now that they have a baby.'

'What? A baby! No, I didn't know that. He did mention his girlfriend to me, but I thought it was just a fling, like his other girlfriends. Now I know why he hasn't been responding to my emails. He's too busy changing nappies, I assume,' she says with a loud laugh.

'And Ed is busy with his studies and his cricket. He doesn't visit often, but he's thinking of coming down for Christmas. Marg and Wayne are so very proud of him, and very excited about his trip to London. They may even go up with him,' continues Marlene.

'Well, please give them my love, Mum.'

'I will, Aida. You look after yourself now. Love you.'

'Love you too, Mum.'

There's a knot in her heart as she puts down the phone. Her mum has never told her she loves her. This is the very first time. She replays this over and over in her head.

'She does love me. Wow! Oh, Mum, I miss you so much,' she says out loud. 'And Max has a baby. Goodness, that was a quick move.' She chuckles to herself.

And with these happy thoughts, her mind escapes to little Alex.

'Goodnight, Alexi.'

******

Chapter 34

Surprisingly, just as her life seems to be happy and comfortable, it is to take another disastrous turn.

Aida receives an early phone call from Max to come home quickly.

'Aida. You need to come home, now,' he says. 'It's your mum. I can come and pick you up if you like.'

'No, Max. I have a car now. Is she alright? Is she ill? Are you back home?'

'Yes, I got here yesterday. Drive carefully. But please hurry. See you soon.'

And with that, he hangs up, purposely ignoring her questions.

She's worried, so she telephones her mum, but she doesn't pick up the phone. She tries again. No answer. *What on earth could have happened?* She tries Sandy's phone, and also no answer.

What on earth has happened now? she thinks.

Pensively, she packs a few clothes, grabs her keys, and makes a quick call to Joan to let her know she won't be at work, and heads for the freeway.

The radio keeps her company. She would normally sing along to the familiar tunes, but her heart is not into singing today, so she turns the dial to talkback station, just to have something in the background.

It's her first time back home since her move and she marvels at the beauty surrounding her as she leaves the city behind and heads up through the countryside. Not as green as she expected, but then it is summer and the harsh sun has taken a toll on the open farmlands. A smile creeps over her face as she approaches Glenrowan for a break and quick bite to eat. She calls her mum again. But still no answer. She tries Max's phone, but he also doesn't pick up. She worries as she resumes her trip.

'Not far now,' she whispers. 'Whatever could have happened?'

Her worry increases as she gets closer, but she dismisses it as she concentrates on her driving and the scenery.

The road takes her through Myrtleford and onto Tawonga and she knows she is getting close. With the car window now fully wound down, she breathes in the fresh air as she turns left into Edge Street from the main road.

A twitch of anxiety seizes her, as she sees a small gathering of people in front of her home, with Max standing by the roadside. There are two police cars and an ambulance parked in front of her house. Her heart sinks and her anxiety increases. She awkwardly parks her car on the curb and gets out. Max quickly rushes to her.

'Don't go in, Aida. Let the police finish their work,' begs Max, as he pushes back on her shoulders.

Sandy tries to block her too, but she forces herself through. Detective Blyth sees her and stops her and, holding her arm, he guides her up the steps and into the lounge and sits beside her. A female officer also sits to her left. Her heart is beating faster than ever and her face is scrunched up in worry.

'Where's Mum? Where's my mum?' she asks, nudging the officer's hand off her back.

She doesn't notice Sandy and Marg by the lounge door, trying to hide their tears.

'I'm so sorry, Aida. Sandy and Marg had not heard from her for a few days, and Sandy could not get in touch with her by phone, and we were called. Unfortunately, there has been a tragedy. Marlene tried so hard to deal with her pain. The loss of a husband and the disappearance of a young child is too much for anyone to deal with. We found her in the shed.'

With hands over her face, and heart racing, Aida wails. Finding it hard to breathe, instead of slumping onto the couch, she stands up and Sandy rushes to put her arms around her and cries with her.

Aida knows what has happened. Detective Blyth does not need to say it. Catching her breath, she waves the air around her face with both hands, and fidgets on the spot. She leans on Sandy as they embrace, both crying uncontrollably. Max looks on, hands in his pockets, feeling helpless. Marg and Wayne are hanging about just in case Aida needs them. She briefly looks out for Ed, hoping, perhaps wishing he is with his parents, but he's not, and she then collapses back onto Sandy.

She waits patiently as the officers and the coroner complete their work.

'I want to see her please.'

'No, not now, Aida. You will get a chance to see her when she is released from the coroner's rooms. I will come and get you when they're done,' says Detective Blyth.

He, himself, also only just managing with the pain, inflicted on this poor family once more.

And with that, she watches as her mother's body, secured in a black body bag, is carried away on a stretcher. And all the memories of that night, so many years ago, come back to her, just as she remembers her father's body on a similar stretcher being taken away.

In her mind, a loud BANG sounds out, as loud and as shattering as it was that night. She hears her mother's pleas to Viktor, to no avail.

No one saw the little five-year-old kneeling on the stairs that night, looking out through the rails, as her father was wheeled out. They all thought she was upstairs, asleep in bed. But she wasn't. She saw it all. A frightened and confused little girl, thinking her daddy was asleep.

She walks up the stairs to her room. Untouched. Exactly as she left it. She ventures into Alex's room, also untouched. But she doesn't go into her mother's room.

******

Chapter 35

Yet another funeral to organise. This one even more solemn than her father's. Alone. Scared. Shocked. Only a small gathering this time. She doesn't have her mother's arm around her shoulders, nor does she have her hand cradled in Edna's. Brave faced, she goes through the motions and is then driven home.

Sandy and Max arrive before her and wait in the kitchen. She can hear their light whispering, not wanting to disturb her, but she composes herself and goes in. Her arms wrapped around herself, leaning on the bench, staring out the window, just as her mother did all those years ago. She stares at the reflection in the glass: a tall, slender woman with dark circles around her eyes, red and swollen, just like her mother's were. She tucks the straggly strands of wavy auburn hair behind her ears and stares at the mirror image of Marlene. She turns to Sandy. She can sense that Sandy too is seeing the same image.

She has so many questions, but the answers will be useless she thinks. She doesn't know whether to feel sorry or sad. Probably both. Marlene was strong, yet so helpless to think that ending her life was her only option. And Aida? She said she loved her. How could she have done this if she said she loved her? What is she to do now?

'She said she loved me the last time I spoke to her on the phone. She said she did.'

Sandy goes to her, but Aida pushes her back. She doesn't have the strength for any emotion right now. She quietly pulls the chair out from under the table and sits down, with Sandy sitting opposite her.

'Mrs Robinson next door can't make it, Aida. She struggles walking now. I'm sure she'll catch up with you some other time,' says Sandy.

Aida nods.

Waiting patiently in the lounge, Marg and Wayne make their way into the kitchen, as Sandy prepares a fresh pot of tea.

'Ed is on his way, love,' says Marg, as she cradles Aida's hand in hers.

Her sad face is unbearable to look at, so Aida stares past her, through the window and into the woods. The beautiful woods she treasures.

'Thank you, Marg.'

The conversation goes cold. Marg and Wayne leave first, followed by Sandy and Max.

'Yell out if you need anything,' says Max, as he gives her a kiss on the cheek before they leave.

With permission from the council, Marlene's ashes are scattered in Kiewa River, as were Nick's ashes almost seventeen years ago.

'They're together now,' she says to Sandy.

'Yes, they are, Aida. They're together now.'

Returning to her mother's home, she ponders on what's happened. Her life seems to pass by as she glances around the kitchen, then looks through the window. Nothing has changed. She can see the woods through the leaves of the Japanese maple. Children playing on the road, and riding through the path, yelling and laughing just like she used to do as a child. She retreats to the hallway and glances up the stairs before making her way into the lounge room. Does she have regrets for leaving her mum? Of course she does. But these thoughts are not going to help her now. She dozes off on the couch, just as the sun comes down on yet another crisp summer's day.

Knock. Knock.

'Hello.'

She hears Ed's voice through her light sleep.

'Come in, Ed,' she says, as she hears the front door creak open.

They hug and she cries. He lets her lean on him for as long as she wants, eventually retreating to the couch. With legs tucked under and cushions pulled up against their bodies, they talk for hours. Catching up on everything that they have done and achieved. Now a qualified solicitor, he tells her he is thinking of moving back to Mount Beauty.

'Jack has offered me a position with his business as a junior partner, hoping I can take over when he retires.'

With eyelids drooping from tiredness, Aida twitches, adjusting the cushions to help her stay awake, and to make herself a little more comfortable.

'Isn't that great, Aida? I can work here back home, where I belong. Oh, I so missed our little town. Did you?'

'I sure did. I thought I was happy mingling and living a corporate life, but deep down my roots are here. This is my home.'

'So, what are you going to do now?' he asks.

'Oh, I'll have to think about that for a while. I have almost finished my course. My boss Joan is encouraging me to complete it. She thinks I'm a natural,' she says with a little smirk.

'And you should,' agrees Ed. 'You certainly are a natural. You will do well in that field. You look so tired, Aida. I'll leave you to rest and I'll pop in tomorrow.'

'Thank you, Ed.'

She sighs as they embrace. She rests her head on his chest, before he gives her a kiss on her forehead and closes the door behind him.

He arrives mid-morning the next day as promised, with a plate of sandwiches. They settle on the couch and their talking continues. But she is still so tired, and unwillingly she dozes off to sleep. Placing a throw over her, Ed moves to the armchair and scours over the local paper, before he too dozes off to have a quick nap.

They wake when they hear a knock on the door.

It's Max, and a young lady carrying a small child in her arms.

'Aida. Ed.'

Max gives Ed a tight handshake and a warm embrace. He then reaches out to Aida and kisses her and also gives her a tight hug.

'This is Beck. You remember me mentioning her to you?' he asks. 'And meet little Josh. Josh Taylor,' he says, smiling and staring at his little boy.

'Oh, wow, Max,' says Aida, quite surprised. She moves closer to Beck to give her a hug.

'Nice to meet you, Aida. Max is always talking about you.'

'Congratulations. I'm so happy for you. Yes, I do remember Max telling me about you, Beck. So pleased to meet you finally. And little Josh looks so much like you, Max. Let me hold him,' she says, as she gently grabs Josh from Beck's arms.

'We've actually come to say goodbye. We are heading back home to Brisbane. I work in Beck's family business and we need to be back by Monday. I would have loved to stay longer to spend time with you. I may not see you both for a while, as it gets quite busy this time of the year, but you will visit, won't you?'

'Of course we will, Max. What about your mum? Will she go up too?' asks Aida.

'I've asked Mum to come with us, but she says she's happy here. And I know she is. This is her home. Best for her to stay here.'

'Yes, she is happy here, Max. And don't worry, I'll keep an eye on her,' reassures Aida.

Little Josh is sat on the rug. Aida sits down next to him, takes out the big toy box under the coffee table and goes through it to find an appropriate toy for him to play with. She chooses the Lego pieces, and Ed joins her on the floor. Aida looks at Ed and he gets teary, remembering how he and Alex used to play with the Lego blocks themselves when they were young.

They talk, laugh, shout and talk some more. Alternating between the kitchen and lounge, they talk till little Josh cries for his meal, signalling it's time for them to leave.

'Are you going to be alright, Aida?' Max asks with genuine concern, as he gets up to leave.

'I'll be fine, Max. We'll keep in touch, I'm sure. You'll have to visit when you can.'

'And you too,' he replies.

A long hug between them seems to signify the end of a long-lasting friendship, one they both hold dear. It seems all the years as children, growing up and playing together, flash past her and she has tears in her eyes.

'Please keep in touch, Max. I'm going to miss you. Love you,' she says wholeheartedly, as she slowly loosens her grip.

'Love you too, Aida.'

And with that, they release their hug and Max and Beck, with little Josh in her arms, make their way out the door.

'Well. That was a surprise.'

'Yes,' replies Ed. 'She found out she was pregnant, so he did the right thing by her, his mum said. It's sad that he's moved to Brisbane. I know his heart is set here in Mount Beauty. He will surely miss his mum as she will miss him.'

The chatter between Ed and Aida continues well into the night. They scrounge around the cupboards to conjure up a meal, with the little ingredients at hand. They laugh and cry and reminisce about all the times she followed him around like a little shadow. He laughs, and tells her how happy he was that she did. She was his only connection to Alex, missing him every day.

And then all of a sudden, he jumps off the couch.

'Hang on a minute, Aida. I'll be right back. I just need to go home and get something.'

He's back in two minutes, and has both hands behind his back.

'Now, please don't get upset. I have something for you.'

With his eyes transfixed on hers, he slowly brings his arm around from behind his back. In his hand is Alex's teddy bear, Flops.

She screeches a loud scream and he grabs her. She is shaking. Both hands rushing to her mouth, Ed reaches up, pulls them down and puts Flops into her trembling hands. She looks up at Ed and pulls Flops to her face, close to her nose, smelling every inch of him.

'What? How do you have Flops?'

'When Alex was taken, he must've dropped him. Flops was on the road. There was so much commotion that night that I decided to take him home, in safe keeping for when Alex got back. The days, weeks and years passed, and I never got to give it back to him, plus I thought that Marlene would not be happy that Flops was not with Alex, that's why I never gave him back. I always believed Alex would come home. So, you can have him, Aida. He belongs to you now.'

'Oh, Ed. This is the best thing you can ever give me. My poor little Alex.'

And with that, she hugs Flops even tighter against her body.

******

Chapter 36

Each day gets better and better. Not to say that Aida doesn't have her bad days. But with Ed by her side, she feels comforted and strong.

She finds it difficult to return to work to hand in her resignation, but Joan understands, and allows her to continue working until she completes her studies. During the last few months of work and schooling, the unit is put on the market and is sold and settled just after finishing her course.

Her farewell is not just farewelling 'another family', as she describes her work colleagues, but another life. One that has allowed her to grow and mature. Her counselling course has taught her skills that she can use and adapt when she feels the need of a guiding hand, or to see life from a different perspective, focussing on the positives, rather than dwelling on negatives. She thanks Joan for her wealth, not just monetary, but the friendship and guidance she has given her — lifetime wealth.

'We will remain friends, won't we, Joan?' she asks, as they hold hands tightly when she says goodbye.

'Of course we will, Aida. And I'll be coming up during my break. Check out that beautiful place you always brag about and call home.'

As she closes the door of the unit behind her for the last time, she thinks of Grandma Edna, almost now believing that her path was laid out for her, without even realising it. Entering as a young lady and now leaving as a grown woman. It isn't with sadness that she turns her back to take the long drive home; it is with contentment that she was given the opportunity to experience a different life to country living, but most importantly, an acknowledgement that she has achieved so much.

The sale of the unit gives her good financial grounding, and she settles into Mount Beauty comfortably, making little renovations to the house where needed, conscious not to change too much of the front of the house. Her mother's words still ring in her ear: 'Alex needs to be able to find his way home, that's why we can't move'.

'I don't want to change too much, Ed, just in case Alex returns. He needs to recognise the house. Just like Mum would want.'

With Sandy keeping an eye on her, and Marg, Wayne and Ed also close by, she feels safe. And Mrs Robinson next door has also been supportive, as supportive as she can be. Now that she has reached her senior years, and living on her own since Mr Robinson's death, it's Aida who keeps on eye on her.

'Goodnight, Alexi.'

'Goodnight, Aidie.'

She hasn't let go of her nightly ritual to Alex, her little brother, so dear to her still, especially now that she has settled back home. And every night she falls asleep soundly, cuddling Flops.

******

Chapter 37

As the years go by, contact with Detective Blyth — Blythy as she still calls him — has almost dried up. His poor health has meant retirement from the police force, and Constable John Brown and his junior partner, Constable Allan Denman, have taken over the Bennet cold case file, as it's now known.

Constable Denman, or Allan as he prefers to be called, pops in.

'We are still onto it, Aida'.

But there are no leads, and the case is cold.

'There has been no new information, Aida. I was wondering if you are prepared to appear on television, just in case some new information comes to hand by the public. Sometimes people may see or hear something that is related to Alex's kidnapping and your father's murder. We hope that someone watching will come up with some detail to reignite the investigation. You know, that happens sometimes. People remember stuff that they thought was insignificant, but lingers in their mind, and then decide to mention it.' He tries to make himself sound hopeful.

'I understand,' says Aida, and she does. 'It has been so long now, almost twenty-eight years? I do appreciate you keeping me up to date, Allan. Let me think about that, and I'll let you know.'

She has almost given up that Alex will be found safe and alive, but still there is a slight glimmer of hope that one day, just one day, John or Allan will come for a visit with better news. She is hoping the television alert will spark interest. She waits for something, anything, but the wait is fruitless.

With Ed's encouragement, Aida continues her studies and completes a course in child psychology. She sets her office up in a shared rental in town and secures a few sessions with young children from Mount Beauty, Tawonga and Bright primary schools. She loves the travel to Bright, as it's an escape to breathe in the fresh air around the mountains and down in the valleys. When she's sad she takes a detour to Kiewa River, sits by the edge of the water and talks to her mum and her dad. She feels close to them when she does this. And Alex is there too, sitting beside her, talking to them with her. She relishes this time all to herself.

Blythy visits her, not to give her updates, but to sit at the kitchen table and share a cuppa and home-made cupcakes. The connection he has with her is unbreakable, having endured much heartache himself with frustration in not being able to solve these terrible crimes. Living through the pain Marlene experienced in losing a husband and young child, and then feeling more pain for Aida, when she lost her mother.

'You know, Aida, one day you will find out what happened that night. I know you will. I may not be around, but you will be, to put your mind at rest.'

'I hope so, Blythy. I hope so,' she says, as they sip their tea.

******

It isn't long before Ed moves in with Aida, and together they nurture the love they always had for each other.

'Two peas in a pod,' says Marg to Wayne.

They spend their free days trekking in Mt Bogong or Bright, sometimes camping in Falls Creek, but always eager to return home to Mount Beauty. They both share a love of reading, be it novels or travel books, with Ed now showing a keen interest in landscape photography. They plan to travel overseas one day.

'Not until Alex is found,' she says to Ed. 'With so much beauty around us, you have plenty to photograph here, eh, Ed?'

She knows he's eager to travel, and he is prepared to give her all the time she needs. Perhaps, with time, she may change her mind and they can embark on a world trip, he hopes.

'I would love to go back to England. Visit the little town where I stayed when I went up for the cricket match. It's so beautiful, Aida. We can hire a car and travel around the countryside. There are so many little quaint, chocolate-box villages, and everything is so green. The landscape makes great photography.'

'One day, Ed. One day.'

When the weather permits, Aida spends time in the garden, having reshaped the vegetable patch to accommodate a wide variety of crops; crops that Marlene would be proud of. The solitude in the garden brings her close to Marlene. She loves to find dandelions in amongst the grass, reminiscing how she used to collect and place them on the back steps to give to her mum. Her sadness is always camouflaged by a fake smile, hoping her family, all her family, is at peace.

She is glad the Ed has demolished the shed and in its place has planted a rose garden, dedicated to Marlene. It even has roses from cuttings that Mrs Robinson had given Marlene, so many years ago. And the big surprise hidden in the shed that was supposed to be her birthday present from her mum and dad is assembled at the side of the house. A swing set; just what she wished for on her fifth birthday.

When she feels melancholy, she sits on the swing and gently sways back and forth, her long legs dragging on the long, tough grass.

And as she walks to the back steps, if she listens intently, she can hear her dad's voice.

'Keep at it, Alex; you'll get there, son.'

She hears it as if it were yesterday. She can hear them laughing the same laugh, and can see her mother's face beaming with delight. She can see a little girl twirling around, humming, in total bliss.

Oh, how she wishes that things had turned out differently. But she acknowledges how fortunate she is that she has studied the minds and behaviours of children, and has no doubt this has helped her come to terms, somehow, with the terrible events inflicted on a little five-year-old. Visions that cannot be unseen, voices that cannot be unheard and memories that she can never let go of.

But best of all, she now celebrates her birthdays. After a brief stroll along the banks of the Kiewa River, she returns home to find a fairy cake on the table. The first of December is a date not forgotten. Ed makes sure of that, as he, Marg, Wayne and Sandy watch her blow out her candles.

******

Chapter 38

'Come in, Blythy,' Aida says to Detective Blyth, as she sees him coming up the steps to the front door.

She greets him with her usual light hug, not wanting to squeeze too hard, follows him into the kitchen, and flicks the switch on the kettle.

'So how have you been, Blythy? What brings you here today?' she asks.

'Oh, I'm fine, apart from the fact that I need a new body,' he laughs. 'But there's something that doesn't make sense, Aida,' he says, sipping his tea. 'It's been on my mind for a very long time and I just can't grasp it. You know what it's like when something niggles at you and keeps niggling, and doesn't go away. Your mum said that Viktor was yelling *you didn't say there were two* to Yuri that night. They must've only been expecting one child in the house, not two, but we haven't been able to find out why. John has been reviewing all the files, but nothing stands out that he can grab and run with. Do you remember that? I know you were only little.'

Aida shakes her head. She thinks hard, but looks up at him and says, 'Sorry, Blythy. I can't remember much of that night. But you're retired. You shouldn't be worried about this now. Shouldn't you be leaving this up to John and Allan?'

There's a pause, as both seem to be in deep thought.

'Would it be okay for me to review the notes, or is that not allowed?' asks Aida.

'I don't think John can do that, Aida. I can ask him, perhaps. I don't see why that would be a problem, but you know procedures. Times have changed and things aren't done the same as they were when I was in charge. They're pretty strict with stuff like that now. Or, I'm thinking, what if you sit with John and go over the files together at the station? Then no one will be able to question that. He can say you're helping him with his investigation.'

'Yep. That sounds good, Blythy. I can do that.'

'Good! I'll get John to ring you.'

And just like Blythy said, John contacts Aida and sets up an appointment for the following Saturday.

'All the notes are now computerised and entered into a database, which makes it easy to retrieve individual details, such as names, fingerprints, previous records of crimes of suspects, addresses, ages, features, etc.,' he says, as his fingers busily tap away on his keyboard.

Aida is quite excited that she can peer at John's computer to see what he is looking at.

'So,' he says with a pause, 'let's make a start on your dad. His name was Nick Bennet.'

John goes over all his past; when and where he was born, his parent's details, his brother's details, the schools he attended, sports clubs, friends, addresses of where he lived and his marriage details to Marlene. He then comes to the birth of the children and Aida smiles as she sees Alex's name and hers appear on screen.

'There seems to be nothing sinister or strange about the life he lived. Just a normal person, living a fairly normal life,' says John.

The next file is Marlene's. They go over the same details as Nick's. And again, nothing out of the ordinary. Aida learns a lot about her parents during this exercise. She almost feels she is living in their shoes having their schools, sports clubs, achievements, work places and addresses displayed on screen.

'Gosh. They did so much in their younger years. How did you get all this information, John?'

'We have access to almost everything. And now with the use of computers we can access records that the normal lay person can't. Isn't that great?' replies John enthusiastically.

This is all very interesting to Aida.

They break for coffee, and have a quick chit-chat in the kitchenette before resuming their search.

Next they go over the very little information they have on Yuri and Viktor. Without surnames, and only a brief description of what they looked like that Marlene could remember on that stressful night, they don't have much to go on.

'We have contacted Interpol with their names, descriptions and crime, but nothing has come back, unfortunately. There is just too little information on them. Their names are very common in the Eastern Bloc countries. It doesn't help us not to know whether they are local people or possibly from overseas, who may have come out for a specific reason. Airport departure and entry records that show these names coming into the country in the previous five years before the crime have been followed through and nothing out of the ordinary has come up. This probably tells us they are Australian residents. Who knows? But I may run these again, just to see if anything new is found. You never know. With today's modern technology and various tools at our fingertips, we may discover something new,' says John, shrugging his shoulders. 'We have also been monitoring departures of all people with these names and, again, nothing unusual.

'They may of course have used different names, or even false passports,' he adds. 'The notes in the file indicate that birth certificates went missing during the break-in at your dad's office. It's a possibility that they used these to forge documents to either get out of the country, or be living here in Australia. A bit scary to think that this may be the case.

'Nick's brother Brian and his wife Sherly are also in the clear. Brian was actually surprised that he was interrogated, saying he hadn't seen his brother in such a long time.'

With her hand over her mouth, Aida tries to hide a big yawn.

'You look tired, Aida. Let's call it a day. We've covered a lot of ground today. How about we continue next Saturday, same time? How's that sound?'

'Thanks, John. Really appreciate all the extra personal time you've been putting into this. Yep, next week is fine by me.'

'Well, we haven't given up yet, Aida,' he says, as he shuts down his computer.

He gives her a pat on her arm and opens the door for her, as she picks up her bag and heads home. She feels a little more optimistic. Maybe he's right. With new technology, he may be able to find out more.

'How was it?' asks Ed when she returns home.

'It was exhausting. There is so much information to go over. After a while it all becomes a blur. I had no idea how much effort they had put into it. Well, I'm back there next week. Let's see what that brings.'

The following Saturday soon arrives. Aida arrives with a hot toastie and take-away coffee from the local coffee shop and sits next to the constable, ready for the next round.

'Breakfast,' she says, as she puts everything on the corner of the desk, away from the computer.

'Oh, gee, thanks Aida. Okay. Here we go,' says John, as he grabs the mouse and flicks through the screens. 'These are all the neighbour's interviews. We'll start with the Fernsby's at number eleven.'

'Oh, I don't know whether I should be looking at the neighbour's information,' says Aida. 'That's Wayne and Marg, Ed's parents. They have been so helpful to me.'

'I'll just read you some of the answers that look suspicious or vague and I'll leave the personal details out.'

Aida nods.

'They were in bed, when they heard Marlene's screams and cries for help that woke them. They ran outside to see what was happening, and all they saw was Marlene running up the street, back inside the house and then out again, screaming that they had taken Alex. We have checked everything, Aida. It was Marg that called the ambulance and the police. The initial call from your mother to 000 was incoherent and the operator couldn't make out if it was a legitimate call or not.'

'I didn't expect anything else from Wayne and Marg. They are like family to me. Marg has always looked out for us, especially after that night.'

'So.' He continues. 'The Robinson's at number nine, next door. Also, fast asleep. Mrs Robinson came out, leaving Mr Robinson in bed, to check what the commotion was all about. They were ruled out for anything suspicious. They must've been really lovely people. They had glowing references from all the neighbours.'

'Yes, they were,' agrees Aida, sad that both have since passed away.

'Next is Sandy Taylor. She was also interviewed and nothing out of the ordinary here. All her details were checked. Oh, hang on. There is a question mark next to her partner's name. Why wasn't this filled in?'

John flicks through the screens. Aida looks away as this makes her dizzy.

'Let me check,' he says and, with a scrunched-up forehead, he navigates through screens slowly, stops, and stretches his arm out to reach the paper file sitting on the pile on the corner of his desk. He flicks through the papers, then looks at the screen. He zeros into Max's details and sees a question mark also in the box that asks *father's name.*

'That's odd,' says John. Why are these fields empty? Who filled this information in?'

Aida watches as he hurriedly scrolls through screens. Up, down, new screens, checking and re-checking. He is going through them so quickly she wonders how he can see anything at all.

'The officer who interviewed Mrs Taylor has left the force. That's a shame. But he probably wouldn't remember that long ago even if I could get in touch with him now.'

'Max's father's name is Nick. I know that. Mum and Sandy used to think it was a coincidence both their husbands having the same name. Can't you ask her?' says Aida.

'Yes, of course, I will.'

'I'm sure everything will be fine with her too,' assures Aida. 'She's also like family to us, and Max is one of my dearest friends. You know, we did primary and secondary school together, always in the same class. He's more like a brother to me than a neighbour.'

'Okay. Leave that with me, Aida. So, the Smiths at number three,' he slurs. 'They were also in bed and only came out to the front yard to see what was happening. They saw Marlene running up and down the street, up to the highway, screaming, and saw Mrs Taylor and the Fernsby's, so they went back inside. Nothing unusual there either. The locals in town were also cleared. They were too far away to hear anything that night, apart from the ambulance and police sirens. Found out what actually happened the next day as the news got around.'

Aida nods again. 'I've gotta go John. This is exhausting.'

'No worries, Aida. We'll see you next week, same time?'

'Sure, John.'

With a very worried look on her face, she leaves.

'Ed. Ed,' she calls, as she arrives home.

'Hi, honey. Have you had lunch? There are sandwiches in the fridge.' He sees the worried look on her face. 'What's up? Everything okay?'

'Let's have a cuppa,' she says, and he follows her into the kitchen.

'What do you know about Max's dad?' she asks him.

'Not much. He's never been back, like Sandy says he will. And Mum said that Sandy told her she's not married to him. She had his baby, he was around for a little while, and then disappeared. Why are you asking?'

'Some of the details on the interrogation report are missing on Sandy's file. Max's surname is Taylor. I know this from the school roll. So, if she isn't married to Max's father, that means that Taylor is her surname, not his dad's. I always thought it was Max's dad's surname. So, if Taylor is his mum's surname, what *is* his dad's surname?'

'Are you going to ask her?'

'Oh, I can't do that. If she's never mentioned it, there must be a reason. John said that he'll go over to re-interrogate everyone. Strange, just so strange she never mentioned this. But then again, there was probably no reason to.'

Aida doesn't go in the following week. She rings John and tells him she will wait for his follow-up on the interrogations first.

Ed starts his own online search, looking up names for Sandy Taylor, Max Taylor and Nick Taylor. But nothing comes up. He logs onto Facebook and does a friend search for Max Taylor. Nothing. He searches Deaths, Births and Marriage records and doesn't find anything for any of them. After a long exhaustive search, frustrated, he gives up.

'I can't find anything on Sandy, Nick or Max, online, Aida. I'm sure John will have access to more records. Let's leave it up to him.'

'What about Max's birth certificate? And marriage certificate? They will have his father's name, won't they?'

'They should. Let's see what John finds,' Ed reassures her.

She rests her head on his shoulder and he puts his arm around her, gently stroking her hair.

Aida doesn't forget about John's promise to interrogate everyone. She rings him almost every day.

'Hello?' Aida answers the phone a few days later and it's John.

'Please come in, Aida. I'll run over the information I have collected. If Ed is free, can he come too?'

Both Aida and Ed are in the car and at the police station in a hurry.

'Sit down, please,' John says after he shakes their hands and closes the door behind them.

'Some very interesting information has come to hand, Aida. I don't know how this was missed all those years ago. It is obvious that the officer who filled in these forms didn't complete all the details. He may have intended to, but resigned from the force and moved interstate, and the information was not followed up.

'So here it is. All your immediate neighbours, well, those who could remember back to 1978, said exactly the same as noted on their records. Apart from Ms Taylor. We have found out, from Ms Taylor, that Max's father's name is Nikolai Ivanov. He and Sandy never married. She believes he left Australia when Max was about two years of age, and she thinks he may be in the Ukraine, his birthplace. They moved around a bit after Max was born, and he paid the rent on her rentals, but this stopped a few years after Max was born. This may be the same time he left Australia. She has never seen or heard from him since.

We have retrieved Max's birth certificate that states his father's name is Nikolai Ivanov. Max's registered name is Maksimum Taylor Ivanov.'

Aida is in shock. She turns to look at Ed. Her whole body shaking, she leans on him for support. This is all too much for her to take in. Her mind is racing, trying to make out what all this means, and how it fits in with what happened that night.

John continues. 'His school enrolment shows his name as Max Taylor. I can't understand why he wasn't enrolled with his registered name if they were given his birth certificate. This would have helped us enormously with our investigations back then.'

Aida starts sniffling. She can't believe that Sandy and Max are possibly embroiled in this.

'What does this mean, John?'

'I don't know. I hate to say this, Aida, but it looks like your dad may have been mistaken for Nikolai Ivanov. And reading Marlene's notes they say that Marlene told Detective Blyth that Viktor called your dad *Nikolai* that night. Marlene couldn't understand why they called him that. That's probably why Yuri and Viktor said, "You didn't say there were two". They may have got the wrong house, Aida. They were obviously expecting only one child to be there, and believed that your father Nick was actually Nikolai. But let's investigate this further. The Homicide Squad have been given this information and they are now running with these as a new lead.'

'How long will this take?' asks Ed.

'I don't know. There are a lot of avenues we have to take. I will keep in touch,' he says. 'I'm so sorry, Aida, but it's a lead; finally, we have a lead to go by. We will be speaking with Mrs Taylor again soon. Maybe there is more that she can help us with, we don't know.'

Ed helps Aida stand and helps her walk to the car. This outcome was certainly not expected and she is in shock, as is Ed. It is too much to take in.

'Can we stop by Kiewa River please, Ed?' asks Aida on their way home.

They sit on the riverbank in silence and she lets the gentle ripples sway onto her shoes and over her ankles. She doesn't care that she's getting wet, and Ed doesn't say anything either. She is in a trance, and he lets her be. He imagines all the thoughts swishing around her head.

It is all too much for her to absorb. After twenty-eight years, there may be some hope that they will find out what happened to Alex. They're thrust into a world of uncertainty, still with so many unanswered questions.

Detective Blyth visits. His walking stick clunks on the porch boards as he approaches the front door.

'Hi, Blythy,' says Ed, as he helps him in.

He coughs to clear his throat as he enters the kitchen and sits at the end of the table, in his usual spot, panting, almost out of breath.

'It's all my fault, Aida. I should've checked everything. It's my fault,' he repeats with his hands shaking on his lap. He looks down, not having the heart to look her in the eyes.

She walks up to him and puts her arms around his shoulders, and shakes him a little.

'You couldn't do everything, Blythy. You had enough to organise. It was just an oversight. The officer who carried out the interrogations should've followed through. These things happen.'

She comforts him. And then he starts to cry.

Aida has never seen an old man cry, apart from her grandpa Bill who had watery eyes when he came for her father's funeral.

She hands him a tissue, and pulls her chair up beside him.

'John will do everything to have this case closed, Aida. I won't rest until it is. Until we find out what's happened to Alex.'

With his hands still shaking, he gets up to leave. Ed helps him down the steps and into his car.

There is an eerie feeling around the house after that information comes to hand. Every time the phone rings, Aida jumps up to answer it, and she's annoyed when it's her friends calling for a chat. She is hanging out for John to ring and give her the good news that Alex is found.

Late one night, as Aida and Ed are on the couch watching television, there is a knock on the door. This time Sandy doesn't call out like she usually does. She waits for the door to be opened.

'Oh, Sandy, come in,' says Ed, surprised. 'Is everything alright?'

She follows Ed into the lounge room, takes a seat on the armchair and starts to cry. Aida stands up.

'I should probably have said something, Aida, but I was afraid, so afraid. I did think that perhaps they may have had the wrong house when Marlene told me that they called your father Nikolai. I didn't know what to think or say. I was scared they may have come back and taken Max.'

She is crying uncontrollably and her body is shivering.

'I am so sorry if it was the wrong house, Aida. I didn't know Nick well, and after I got pregnant, he was a different person to the Nick I knew whilst we dated. He disappeared, Aida. When Max was a toddler, he just took off and left, without a word. Maybe he was in some sort of trouble. Maybe that's why he wanted us to move so many times. Who knows? Oh, Aida. I am so sorry.'

She cries even louder and blows her nose into her wet hanky.

'Have you told Max?' asks Aida.

'Yes, I have. He is beside himself. He can't get his head around everything. He said he will ring you when he can. I guess he needs to process all this information before he does. It is a shock to him, too.'

'Sandy. No one can change the past. We just now need to find out what happened to Alex. I'm sure that Constable John will do everything he can,' says Ed. 'Have you told him everything you know?

'Yes, of course. I'm so sorry, Aida. I'm so sorry. I am to blame for everything. And your poor mum.'

She cries even louder, as she looks down at the floor.

'You didn't know that would happen, Sandy. No one did. You certainly couldn't have stopped it. But why didn't you say something afterwards? We may have had a better chance in finding Alex. Something could've been done then, before the trail got cold.'

Sandy cries louder; her body still trembling. Ed can see that Aida is getting upset. She tries hard to hold her composure and Ed can see this too.

'Have you told the constable everything? Are you sure there is nothing else you need to tell him? Surely you would know Nick's family or acquaintances? Have they been interrogated?' Aida raises her voice, angry at the situation and angry at Sandy right now.

She has so much going through her head, she shoots question after question at Sandy. Trying hard to not let her anger get a hold of her, she wonders if Sandy knew all along that they *did* have the wrong house and questions why she kept quiet about it. She takes long deep breathes as she tries to calm her nerves.

'Aida, can you make us a cuppa please?' Ed asks firmly, signalling her to go to the kitchen.

As Aida walks off, Ed kneels in front of Sandy, takes her hands in his, and looks straight into her eyes.

'Sandy. Listen. It's probably best not to mention it again. Let's move on and see what Constable John digs up. Please try to think of anything you can that may help him solve this. That is the best you can do right now.'

******

Chapter 39

The investigation goes cold, again. With all the efforts that John and the homicide team put into it, the new leads prove nothing. They come to another dead-end.

John visits Aida and Ed with the latest conclusion as to what may have happened that night.

Sitting close to the table, he opens up his briefcase and takes out the many folders and notebooks that make up the Bennet's case; now an all too familiar site for Aida. It frightens her that with so much information collated and investigated there are no leads in finding out what happened to Alex that night and why.

'So, Aida and Ed. Without proof, it appears that the events of that night may have been due to mistaken identity. This conclusion is purely based on information we now have at hand, that Nikolai Ivanov has a Russian name, similar to Yuri and Viktor and the fact that they only expected one child in the house, making us believe that it was Nikolai and Max they were after, and a possibility that is was not your father and Alex they wanted. Once again, there is no proof of this, but just judgement, based on what we know, and the fact that Marlene said they called your father Nikolai and not just Nick.

'When we form a picture from what your mother told us of that night, how they panicked, how they were fidgety and yelling, calling your father Nikolai, asking why there were two children and not one as expected, it may be that things got out of control, and they didn't know what to do. Also showing us that they were not true professionals in child kidnapping, or whatever they set out to do. It can be established that Max's father disappeared, possibly because he knew these people were after him, for whatever reason. And because they couldn't find him, in retaliation, they decided to abduct his son.

'In conclusion, we believe that Max's father is probably dead or hiding somewhere. If he is dead, it probably explains why he has never returned, but if he is in hiding, he is probably wanting these people to believe he is dead, so as to protect his family. With regards to what may have happened to Alex, I believe that after they realised they had the wrong child, Alex may have been raised, or sold, to another family, either here in Australia, or overseas. Seeing that his birth certificate and other certificates were stolen from Nick's office, they may have needed them to use for his new identity.'

Aida is struck with fear and can't ask any questions. She lets Ed do the talking.

'But if the certificates with Alex's name are produced, surely someone will know of him, and the police would find records of these?' asks Ed.

'Yes, true. That's where I think they may have used the original certificates and falsified them by changing some details on them. It would take an astute eye to notice a name change, especially if these are copies and not the originals. He could easily be enrolled in school with a copy of a certificate with a different name on it. You have to understand that back in the seventies school record taking was not as stringent as it is now.'

Aida is shaking. What if Alex is living close by? What if he has been taken overseas, to Russia perhaps? How can she ever find him?

'Do you think, John, that they would have killed him, once they discovered he was not the right child?' asks Aida in a soft voice.

Ed grabs her hand and squeezes it hard.

'Oh, Aida. Don't think that. I don't think anyone would harm a small child,' Ed says to soothe her.

John takes a loud, deep breath. 'There is always that possibility, but I'd like to think not.'

It's all too much for Aida. She bursts into tears and runs upstairs to her bedroom, slamming the door shut.

Silently, the constable packs up all the paperwork strewn across the table, packs it neatly into his case, gives Ed a firm handshake and leaves.

******

2008

With the cold teacup still in her hands, and the wind picking up, she slides off the porch rail and turns around to head inside. But from the corner of her eye, that image is in front of her again. Blue jeans, sloppy t-shirt, black sneakers, arms hanging loosely by his side. He is standing across the road in front of the house, staring at her.

She turns to face the man and studies his face. Round, rugged, with thick dark hair cut short, rimless glasses sitting close to his forehead and an inquisitive expression on his brow, just like hers. Their eyes lock into each other's, almost impossible to unlock. This time he doesn't turn right to head for the town. He walks across the road and stops as he gets close to the letterbox. He stares at the weathered street number painted on it, looks up at her and freezes.

Her cup falls as both hands rush to her mouth to silence her gasp, and tears start to well in astonishment and disbelief.

The drop of her cup alerts Ed, who is on his computer in the lounge room. He makes a dash to the front door, flings open the fly-wire screen, halts and then walks slowly toward her. With both his hands on her face, he tries to turn her head to face him, but her neck is stiff, still looking at the man standing in front of her letterbox. Ed turns to also have a look. He squints. He seems to vaguely recognise him, and even though there are slight doubts, these are dismissed as he stares at him a second longer.

He scans his body, taking in his physique, his facial features and the resemblance of someone familiar.

The seconds they stare at each other seem like a lifetime. Aida is still frozen as Ed steps down from the porch and inches closer to him. His eyes still scanning every inch of him, as if trying to place puzzle pieces together. It seems this person is doing the same. Ed looks at his eyes under his rimless glasses, his nose, his thin lips, chin and pale skin. His shoulders are broad. And then his eyes go to his hands; both down, limp by his side. Instantly Ed's eyes are drawn to something on his face — something he is half expecting. The skin, shiny and tight under his bottom right eyelid, slightly stretched and pulled down. His eyes go up to his eyebrow; a scar running across the middle of it, separating the brow into two. He looks down at his hand, also sporting a faint scar that runs up the wrist to his arm.

After some deliberation, almost in disbelief, they inch closer towards each other. The magnetic pull is too hard to break and they immediately embrace. Neither of them want to let go, but they do, just to look into each other's eyes again, before the hug recommences in earnest.

Aida takes her time to join them, stiff and statuesque, cautious, silently questioning if this is real.

But it's Alex that makes the move to go to her first, grabs her in his arms and squeezes her so hard, almost crushing her, and whispers Aidie in her ear.

They cry on each other's shoulders for ages, a whole thirty years' worth, as he soothes her hair over and over.

The moment is uncanny. It brings mixed emotions, as they've waited for this for so long. As she absorbs his warmth, her thoughts rush to her mother and father.

'Rest in peace, Mum and Dad,' she whispers to herself. 'He's home.'

******

Chapter 40

Alex can't believe that he is actually walking up the front steps, onto the porch and into the hallway. His eyes look up at the staircase and then the lounge as Ed leads the way and invites him to sit on the sofa. Aida follows behind them. But before sitting, they cry. They hug. Aida can't let go of him, and Alex doesn't want to let go of her. The moment is surreal. Ed stands back to allow them to rejoice this long-awaited reunion. Crying turns to sobs. Alex then turns to Ed for a long embrace. Tears stream down their faces. They take their glasses off to wipe their eyes and noses and then embrace again. Aida fidgets on the spot, waiting her turn to hug him again. She can't believe what is happening and she's shaking. Her mind races with so many thoughts and questions.

'Sit down, Alex,' says Ed, pointing to the couch.

Kneeling on the floor in front of him, Aida tilts her

head up to gaze at him and puts her hand on his knee. He grabs it and cradles it. They all talk over each other, giggling and fidgeting as the excitement grips them. Not exactly knowing what to do or what to say.

Ed takes a deep breath.

'How did you get here, Alex?'

'I had to use my navigator, to find the address. When I saw Aida on the porch this morning, I was too scared to come up to the house. I knew it was you sitting on the railing,' he says.

He looks at her and squeezes her hand harder.

'It was like I was staring at Mum. I was so overcome with emotion I couldn't stop, so I walked on, to get a hold of myself. I sat on the park bench on the edge of town, even too frightened to venture in; scared that I might see Dad's office. I sat there until I gathered enough courage to come back. You know, I have gone over and over this moment so many times. I never thought it would be this hard.'

Tears well in his eyes as he recounts his return, his hands shake and his voice chokes up.

As he talks, Aida focuses on his face, the resemblance to the six-and-a-half-year-old little boy very evident. His eyes sparkle, lit up with tears of joy. The scars visible, but set as if they were always there. His skin clear, not tanned as it was when he was a child, and she sees a strong resemblance to her father.

She can hardly believe he is here. She kneels up and touches his face. He removes his glasses to wipe his eyes and she runs her finger over the scar on his eyebrow.

'Yes, Aida. It healed, eventually,' he says with a little nervous chuckle.

'How did you find us?' asks Ed.

Alex takes a deep breath.

'Well. It wasn't easy. I always knew I had another family, and I always felt that the life I was living was only temporary and that one day I would be back home. But as I grew, it became harder and harder to break away from my new family.'

Aida looks down and shuffles to make herself comfortable on the floor in front of him, before locking her eyes back onto his.

'Once the Internet came, it became easier for me to start my search. Mama Daria encouraged me to search for my real parents. You see, they adopted me, Mama Daria and Papa Dima. As I grew, I began calling them Ma and Pa, even though I knew I had another mum and another dad. I spoke about you all the time in the beginning. But as the years passed, I became accustomed to my new life and my new parents, and you became distant — not lost, just distant.'

He squeezes Aida's hand tighter and clears his throat.

At this point, Aida starts crying and has to leave the room. She runs into the kitchen. Alex stops talking and Ed puts his arms around his shoulders. They both take a deep breath to wait for Aida.

'Why don't we go into the kitchen,' says Ed.

As they make their way to Aida, Alex can't help but look around the lounge room. He briefly looks at the photos on the mantle and the dresser. He wants to go up close to get a better look, but holds back. Pain starts to creep in, so he moves on, and follows Ed.

He glances up at the stairs, almost recounting each step as his eyes reach the top landing, quickly looks away and then nervously heads into the kitchen.

Aida is wiping her eyes as they enter.

'Are you alright?' asks Ed, as he puts his arm around her waist.

She nods.

'Are you okay, Aidie?' says Alex.

She nods and instantly runs to hug him.

'I never thought I'd hear you call me that ever again,' she says to Alex.

'I never forgot you, Aidie. Never!'

Ed puts the kettle on and reaches into the top cupboard for a box of biscuits. All three are still in disbelief that they are together.

'But how did you get here, Alex?' asks Ed.

'I parked my car a few blocks up, behind the woods, just in case I changed my mind,' he says, a little embarrassed.

Ed smiles as he continues with the tea. 'Where have you come from? You have an accent that I can't quite make out.'

'I've been staying in Myrtleford for a few nights, planning my drive here. But I've actually flown in from Heathrow. I stopped in Melbourne to recover from the flight and then took a hire car here. You see, I've been planning this reunion for many years.

'We moved to London from Belarus just before I started senior school and settled in Camden. Mama is a school teacher and can speak English, and Papa drove a taxi, until he got sick. Mama wanted a better education for me, hence the move. Initially, I could only speak English. It was good that Mama could communicate with me and then taught me to speak Russian.'

Aida listens intently, as she tries to form a picture of his life and compares it to the life her mum and her were living here, whilst worrying about what may have happened to him. She tries hard not to think that he was getting on with his life, whilst they were suffering so much pain. How could his new parents not know about his kidnapping?

He takes a seat at the table and clasps his hands together, rubbing them as he gathers his words.

'I never forgot our school, Mount Beauty Primary, and of course my family and you, Ed, and our cricket games. I missed you all so much, for a very long time.'

He turns to Aida when he says this.

Aida takes a deep breath as she pulls her shoulders back and stiffens up.

'My curiosity in searching for you started when we did Australian studies and that's when my interest really took hold. But I was frightened, so my search was on and off, depending on my state of mind. Mentally, I was making notes of where to start looking, pressing my memory for names and places.

'Once I was strong enough and had the courage, I started the search in earnest. Of course, Google helped a lot. I searched for Mum and Dad first. And it was a good thing I remembered their names — and I certainly remembered my name, even after my new parents named me Alexei.'

He looks up at Aida but she now has her head down listening to every word he is saying, her hands fidgeting on her lap.

'It was a real shock to see their death notices online. It was an even bigger shock to see that Dad was shot and I was abducted. I didn't know I was abducted. This terrified me. I couldn't tell anyone because I didn't want my parents to be in any sort of trouble.'

Aida sniffles.

'I found newspaper articles and researched the whole story, about the shooting and my kidnap. It was all too much for me to grapple with, so I let it go for a while, until I got the urge and built up the courage to continue. I couldn't believe that all of this was happening, whilst I was living a new life halfway across the world in a different country. It was as if it was not me in the articles. I couldn't tell my parents because they believed I was given up for adoption legally. I was too scared to say anything to them. I was scared that they wouldn't allow me to keep searching.'

'How did you find out you were adopted?' asks Ed.

'Just before enrolling into senior school Mama told me. I wasn't surprised. I always felt different, and I didn't look anything like them. And, curiously, I wondered why my English was so good, compared to the other children in class. Initially I thought it was the English that Mama taught me at home, but later, it all made sense, I guess.'

'But what about Yuri and Viktor; the men that took you? The men that shot Dad? What happened to them?' asks Aida.

'I don't know anything about them. I just remember going on a boat and then in an aeroplane. I was sick on the boat. My pyjamas were wet and I was so cold. I must've fallen asleep, because the next thing I remember was when the plane landed. Some people took me for a long drive to my new parents. I never asked them why I was there. I was scared. I cried a lot, calling out for Mum and Dad.'

'Oh.'

Aida is surprised and sad, and reaches for his hand across the table.

'Ed, do you remember a cricket game at Camden? It was around 1995. I was there. I was a spectator.'

Surprised, Ed's face lights up. 'What?'

'I read in our university newsletter that a cricket team from Australia was coming to play at Camden, and I decided to come and watch. I had no idea you were in the team.'

'Oh, far out!' says Ed, still surprised.

'My heart stopped when I was given a leaflet with the names of the players of both teams, and I saw your name. I had to look at it a few times to realise that it was actually you. There couldn't be too many Edward Fernsbys around. I knew immediately it was you, Ed, when you walked out on the field. Shaking in my seat, I watched the whole game, and even cheered for you.

'I wanted so much to approach you when you walked out at the end of the game, which you won, of course, but I was frozen in fear. It's as if my past was coming back to me.'

'Oh, Alex. That would have been unbelievable,' says Aida, feeling his emotions.

'I intended to make contact with you before you returned back to Australia, but I was too scared to approach you. I wasn't sure how I, and you, would react. And then you left.

'After this, I was even more determined to find out more. I continued with my online search for you, Aida, and found you are registered as a child psychologist, with a Mount Beauty address. I knew straight away that I was on the right track. And then, Ed, I looked for you. I was so excited to see you working as a solicitor here in town. And I also found photos of the Mount Beauty cricket team and I picked you out straight away. I wasn't surprised to see you made the team,' he says with a big smile.

Alex drops his head and wriggles in his chair, feeling a little emotional, then looks up at them and continues.

'That was the easy bit. I then had to work out how I was going to tell Mama Daria that I had found you and that I wanted to come to Australia to visit you.'

'And Dima?' asks Aida.

'He passed away a few years back from cancer.'

Alex looks sad as he says this.

'You look tired, Alex. Do you want to rest?' asks Aida.

'No. No. I'm fine,' he replies and takes a sip of tea. 'Oh, this tea is delicious. We don't have nice tea in Belarus, and the English tea is just not the same.'

'What do we do now?' asks Ed. He turns to Aida and asks, 'Should we let John and Allan know?'

'I guess we should,' Aida replies.

'Who are they?' asks Alex.

'Constable John Brown and Constable Allan Denman have been in charge of the investigation trying to find you and your abductors.'

'I see,' replies Alex. 'Yes, I guess we should.'

'Let's finish our tea first,' says Aida.

******

Chapter 41

John can't believe what he is being told. After shaking Alex's hand, he reassures them that his partner, Constable Allan Denman, now in charge of the Bennet's file, will take over the investigation and all the paperwork.

John can't help but feel a new surge of energy, even as he is approaching retirement age. He is relieved that this case is partially resolved before he leaves the force. A case that has been haunting him and Detective Blyth these past thirty years. Brushing his hand through his thinning hair, he stares at Alex in astonishment, captivated by this moment; a moment he deeply and truly believed would never eventuate.

When they return home, Aida encourages Alex to wander up the stairs to his room, which he does with caution, his feelings too strong and his mind racing in anticipation of entering. Aida follows him.

As he enters, he looks around the room and then heads to the window and glances down the street and into the woods. He looks at the pathway, now trodden and flattened by the heavy usage over the years and imagines him and Ed running through to play cricket. He then sits on the side of bed as tears roll down his face.

Aida quickly goes into her room, and returns with Flops.

'Here, Alex. He belongs to you.'

And even with tears in his eyes, Alex manages a laugh as he caresses Flops' ears.

'He fell out of my hands that night. I missed him, especially when I went to bed,' Alex says, stroking him gently.

Aida sits next to him and they hug. With their heads leaning on each other's, they quietly cry. Not a word is spoken. The late afternoon sun retreats behind the clouds, until the room is dim and silent.

Aida stands and kisses the top of his head, then leaves, closing the door gently behind her. With Flops on top of him, Alex lies down on his bed, and closes his eyes.

He wakes up startled and shocked that he actually fell asleep. He didn't realise the emotional toll this day has taken on him. The window, slightly open, lets in the evening wind, softly caressing the curtains. He gets up and puts on the light. He scans his room, still as he left it, some thirty years on. His toys and books are still intact, and on the dresser sits his cricket ball. Worn, the colour faded, when he picks it up and smells it he is taken back to the clearing with Ed. With the ball in hand, he goes to the window and takes a look at the side garden and can hear, 'Like this, son,' in his father's voice, teaching him the spin bowl. He can see his mum sitting on the steps and Aida dancing on the grass. A picture of perfect happiness.

Aida and Ed's whispering from downstairs urges him to join them.

'I didn't realise I was so tired,' he says, as he rubs his eyes with his hand. 'My room is exactly as it was back then.' He giggles.

'Mum didn't want anyone to go in and touch anything,' Aida says with sad eyes, 'but I would sneak in when she wasn't looking and lie on your bed. Are you hungry?' she asks. 'I have some meat pie for you.'

And without waiting for his answer, she places the pie in front of him.

He doesn't reply. His emotions race inside him. He sits down at the table, and slowly starts to eat.

There is no doubt that he is confused and bewildered by the events of the last few days, and starts to realise how much he has missed. His thoughts go to his parents, especially his father, brutally murdered for reasons that are still unexplainable.

His thoughts turn to his mother, who suffered for so long, desperately trying to find her little boy, and in the end paying the ultimate price; just too much for her to bear, that she thought Alex believed she had chosen Aida over him.

And he then looks up at Aida. Now a grown woman, all the years that she too must have suffered, watching and living through all these events and now all by herself. And what about Edna and Bill? How they would have suffered too, not knowing what had happened to him. There are so many thoughts going through his mind, he can't eat the whole pie, and then turns to Ed and places his hand on his arm, almost as a sign for help.

Could he have fought harder out of Viktor's grip? Should he have tried? Should he have escaped and made his way home sooner, at least while his mum was still alive? These unanswered questions throw so much guilt on him and his breathing becomes shallow with anxiety building up inside him.

'Let's retreat to the lounge room,' says Ed, as he senses the tension. 'Come on, mate.'

He puts his arms around Alex's shoulders and they make themselves comfortable on the couch.

******

Chapter 42

It takes a few days for the whole story to be told. Even then Aida remembers other questions to ask, finding it hard to believe that he is actually safe, well and, above all, loved by his new family. But deep down she feels robbed of him. Why should another family have had him, and not his real family? She feels a sense of betrayal — emptiness and pain that could've been avoided, perhaps. Could it have been? Her thoughts turn to Sandy but she quickly dismisses them. Ultimately, there is no one to blame, apart from the murderers and abductors.

Aida is sad that her mother can't experience this moment. The visit to Kiewa River the next day helps to some extent soothe the pain that both Aida and Alex are feeling when they sit by the riverbank.

He cries as he reflects on the pain his mother suffered for so many years as they watch the wreath of flowers they place on the water gently drift downstream.

Everyone in town rejoices when they hear the news.

Ed's parents are ecstatic and it takes them a while to believe it.

Marg greets him like a long-lost son, and her thoughts turn to Marlene. How happy she would be to know that he is home, safe and well.

The phone call to Max is equally jubilant as is the call to Sandy, who has since moved up to Queensland to be close to her family. Her cries of joy screech through the phone, and her voice trembles as she talks with him.

But the most content, if not surprised, to see Alex is Blythy. With John standing by Blythy's wheelchair to support him, they both anxiously wait for Alex and Aida. With his health and eyesight fading, his face lights up as Alex and Aida walk through the glass doors of the nursing home to share the good news with him.

Teary-eyed and with shaky hands, Blythy looks up at Aida and says, 'I told you, Aida. I told you he would be back.'

But Alex's visit is short. After attending numerous meetings with John, Allan, and a sergeant from the Homicide Squad, he makes plans to return back home. Copies are taken of his passport and his driver's licence. It's difficult for Aida to see his name as Alexei Dimitrovik. And even though Aida cannot understand Russian, she can sense the pressure his mother is putting on Alex to return home, when he rings her each night.

'I can't leave her,' he says to Aida in a sad voice. 'I am going to have to tell her about the abduction, now that all the details are confirmed. She doesn't know any of this. No doubt she will have to be interviewed. It will be difficult for her to comes to term with this, and I need to be there to support her through it.'

'I understand,' Aida replies.

But she doesn't. She wants him to be back home, with her, like she has dreamed of.

Ed and Aida want to take him sight-seeing to Bright and Mount Bogong and beyond, but Alex just wants to hang around the house and spend time with them. They look at photo albums of when they were young, and find a photo of his first day at school, standing next to Ed.

'You always towered over me, Ed,' says Alex, laughing. 'I remember that day. Mum had to hold the umbrella over the camera as it started drizzling. We look so happy, eh, Ed.'

He runs his fingers over photos of his mum and dad and then cries, feeling pain for the agony that his mum and Aida were put through all these years not knowing what had happened to him.

The following day they walk across the road through the woods to the clearing. Alex gets teary as he sees a group of young boys playing cricket, reminding him of his matches with Ed. It's all too much for him and they make their way back home. But his sadness turns to laughter as they come to the spot where he had the fall on his bike. Ed joins in with a nervous laugh, as they cross their arms around each other's shoulders, with Aida smiling behind them.

******

Chapter 43

His farewell has mixed emotions. He is happy that he is finally found, but sad that he is leaving.

Silently, Aida screams for him to stay. This is your home. Please don't go, Alex. I want you here with me. I've waited so long for you to return home. Please don't leave me.

Ed puts his arm around her. He knows what she is thinking, and it's painful for him too.

'We'll talk on the phone,' Alex says, as he hugs Aida tight. 'You and Ed can come and visit and stay with us. There are so many beautiful places for you to photograph.'

'Yes, I'm sure there are.' Ed chuckles.

******

After he's gone, Aida recounts his story. She imagines a frightened little boy, ripped from his mother's arm, driven and flown halfway around the world, in a strange country, living with people who all of a sudden are his new parents. Cold, wearing only his pyjamas and Viktor holding him tight, she pictures a frightened little boy, trying to wriggle free, calling out to his parents, and wanting Flops to cuddle.

******

Chapter 44

Ed sprints home. Aida is not answering the house phone or her mobile. He wants to get to her before she puts on the TV to watch the evening news. But he's too late. When he arrives, he sees her glued to the television screen with her hands to her mouth.

'Repeating today's latest news. Seven-year-old Josh Taylor was taken from his home in the Brisbane suburb of Hendra, in the early hours of this morning. His parents, Max and Beck Taylor were woken to commotion in the hallway, but were unable to stop the two masked abductors. Josh is described as thin build, dark hair, wearing blue pyjamas with an elf motif on the front. If anyone has any information as to his whereabouts, or if anyone knows who has taken him, please contact your local police station ...'

******